CU00841966

About the author

Tony Bury, born in 1972 in Northampton, England, has had a passion for writing songs, poems and short stories since an early age. He has taken it more seriously since having kids, writing several children's books and screen plays as well as several adult novels. This is his first children's book.

To Rory
Hope you enjoy the Book

Tony

Ane the Last Witch

Tony Bury

Ane the Last Witch

Nightingale Books

NIGHTINGALE PAPERBACK

© Copyright 2018
Tony Bury

The right of Tony Bury to be identified as author of
this work has been asserted by him in accordance with the
Copyright, Designs and Patents Act 1988.

All Rights Reserved

No reproduction, copy or transmission of this publication
may be made without written permission.
No paragraph of this publication may be reproduced,
copied or transmitted save with the written permission of the publisher,
or in accordance with the provisions
of the Copyright Act 1956 (as amended).

Any person who commits any unauthorised act in relation to
this publication may be liable to criminal
prosecution and civil claims for damages.

A CIP catalogue record for this title is
available from the British Library.

ISBN 978 1 912021 52 9

Nightingale Books is an imprint of
Pegasus Elliot MacKenzie Publishers Ltd.
www.pegasuspublishers.com

First Published in 2018

Nightingale Books
Sheraton House Castle Park
Cambridge England
Printed & Bound in Great Britain

For my niece, Ane, and my
nephew, Owen.

Chapter 1

"Ane Maria!"

Ane could hear the tone in her mother's voice. That, coupled with the use of Ane's middle name, only meant one thing: Ane was in trouble. Her mother would only ever use her middle name when she was in trouble.

Ane often wondered how much trouble she would need to get into for her mother to use their last name as well. She was pretty sure there were a few occasions in the past where she had been close. She had even tried to make it happen on more than one occasion, but to date it had never happened.

Ane looked over at Willow who was curled up on the end of the bed. Willow, was never affected by the bellowing of Ane's name. Not even when it included her second name. Willow had become used to it. Especially over the last few years, as Ane had become more and more curious about the world of magic. Willow remained on the bed licking her paws, anticipating the arrival of Ane's mother. Cats, in general, never really worried about anything, and Willow was the type of cat that never even worried about worrying about anything.

Ane started to tidy up their latest joint magical experiment as quickly as she could. It was in various stages all across her bedroom. Various stages because there was never just one experiment at a time. Ane would start with one, but if it didn't work straightaway she would start another, leaving the first for Willow to finish. Finishing a magic trick rarely happened in Ane's house, waiting for magic wasn't Ane's strongest point.

Ane and her family lived in the same windmill that her grandfather had grown up in. It wasn't hard to miss as it was the only windmill in the street. Her mother had told her that the street had been built around the windmill. The truth was, once, when Ane's grandfather was her age, he had tried a spell to fill the house with flowers for his mother. Unfortunately, something had gone completely wrong with the spell, and the house had turned into a windmill. The mix up had become somewhere between flour and flowers but nobody ever really discovered how. Her grandfather never attempted the trick again. Even though her great-grandmother when she returned home, loved it that much that they decided to keep the windmill. Throughout the years, her grandfather, who still lived with Ane and her mother, had taught her a few tricks about living in the windmill. For example, Ane knew she had some time until her mother would get to her. It had only been the first call. There would usually be more before her mother ventured the sixty-three steps to the first floor where Ane's bedroom was. Her grandfather had told Ane that it would take at least the time it took her to count to one hundred to get from the bottom step to her bedroom. Yes, she still had some time, but Ane started to count in her head nonetheless.

Ane had been working on several experiments since returning from school. All with the same objective: to make an everlasting bag of gummy bears. She was sure it was going to be possible. It was a simple spell. At least, that was what she had told her best friend Owen as they walked home from school together. It was just another simple spell. It will take me ten minutes. She also told him he didn't need to spend his pocket money on sweets any more. She would take care of it. So far, this afternoon she had not quite taken care of it.

There was a moment when one of the red ones, her favourite flavoured gummy bear, briefly came to life and chased Willow around the room. That had been exciting. Ane eventually manage to catch it, and quickly returned it back to its original form. Unfortunately, before she had the chance to eat it, Willow stole the gummy bear, took it into the bathroom, and flushed it down the toilet. Willow strutted back to the bed and had been lying there, pleased with herself, ever since.

Ane continued to tidy up her equipment. She knew her mother would be cross at the magic experiment she had set up in her bedroom. There were rules in the house with regards to magic. They weren't extensive rules. In fact, there was just one rule in the house to do with magic: **no magic!**

It was very difficult for Ane to stick to this rule, especially as it only applied to her. That wasn't fair. Her grandfather, who Ane knew was an amazing wizard, maybe not as good as one of The Great Wizards, but amazing none the less. Spent most of his time in the basement on one spell or another, and he hardly ever got into trouble. Ane didn't even know if he had a middle name. Her grandfather was fun. He always allowed Ane to help him with his spells, but mainly when her mother wasn't around to see them.

Ane's mother was also a witch, a very good witch. Although, for some reason unknown to Ane, she didn't want to practise it any more. She only ever seemed to use magic when she was cleaning up after Ane. Ane still took every opportunity to point this out to her mother; that that was a daily use of magic too.

Ane petitioned her mother on several occasions about the reversal of this rule. In fact, at one time she had three hundred and two signatures on the petition. Her mother had known that they were in Ane's and Owen's handwriting, but she had applauded the effort. The ban on magic, however, wasn't lifted. Ane's mother pointed out that you needed at least two thousand signatures to be taken seriously. Ane had managed to get to seven hundred and twelve before her wrist had started to ache, and she had become bored with the whole petition.

"Ane Maria!"

That was the second call. Depending on how much trouble she was in, she didn't know if there was going to be a third call. Ane collected everything as fast as she could and threw it all under the bed. It was the quickest way of tidying up. As the last piece went under the bed she heard footsteps. Her mother must have been at least halfway up the stairs already when she had called her. Another thing that her grandfather had taught her was that with a windy staircase you can only hear steps around step thirty-four. Whatever she had done, it was a two-call problem. That wasn't a good sign. Ane jumped on the bed as Willow jumped off and went and sat in her bed in the corner of Ane's room. She knew that was far enough away from where all the action was going to be.

Ane grabbed the book off the side and pretended to read it. Then remembering quickly, she took off her witch's hat and threw it behind the bed as the door flew open.

Ane didn't look up from her book. Actually, she raised it a little higher as the footsteps came closer.

"Ane Maria, what is the one rule in this house?"

Ane peered over the top of the book.

"Sorry, Mother? I was just reading."

Ane lifted the book a little higher again. Ane's mother took the book, turned it the right way around, and gave it back to Ane. Ane lifted it a little higher still so her mother couldn't see the smile on her face. It was a silly mistake, and she knew that her mother did that just to prove the point she wasn't really reading.

"I said, Ane, what is the one rule we have in this house?"

Ane held her breath and looked up at her mother as if to show her that she was thinking about what the rule was. With that, her mother whipped the book out of her hands and placed it on the side.

"The one about brushing my teeth? I did, I swear…"
Ane smiled the biggest smile she could to show her
mother her teeth, hoping there were no gummy bears still
stuck in them. The look on her mother's face told Ane
this wasn't one of those deflective moments that her cute
smile could get her out of.

Her mother just stood there looking at her waiting
for a response. She could always wait Ane out, and Ane
knew this. She had tried a few times to take her on. Her
record was one hour and twenty-two minutes, but in the
end Ane always lost against her mother. Her grandfather,
however, would give in after a few minutes. One cute
smile, and he was putty in her hands.

Eventually Ane said the words she knew she had to.

"No magic?" Ane tried to say it in the softest voice
she could. One that reminded her mother that she was still
her little, cute and adorable daughter.

"That's right, no magic, and what have you been
doing up here for the last hour?"

Ane wanted to say reading. The words were there,
right on the tip of her little tongue. The R was rolling
around her mouth. At the last minute she decided not to
though; she knew deep down she wasn't going to get
away with it. Her mother knew. Ane didn't know how,
but she always knew when Ane had been playing with
magic.

"But, Mum, I was just…" Ane didn't get the chance
to finish the sentence.

"I can guess what you were just, Ane Maria. Come
with me!"

The double-barrelled name continued. That was still a bad sign. Ane couldn't think what she had done to make her mother this upset. All the spells she had cast over the last couples of days were running through her head. Every one of them had been returned to normal and she had already been told off for them. Surely, she couldn't be told off twice for the same spell? That wasn't really fair.

This was nearly a three-named telling-off, she could feel it. Ane got off the bed and followed her mother down the stairs. Ane tried to walk step by step with her mother, but she was struggling to keep up. That was another bad sign. Her mother was in a rush, which told Ane that whatever had happened was probably still happening. As they reached the bottom step she could hear her grandfather laughing. When they entered the kitchen, her grandfather picked up the paper, and hid behind it. Ane checked to see if he had the paper the right way up, just to make sure he didn't get in trouble too. He had. Ane's mother turned to look directly at Ane.

"Do you have anything to say, young lady?"

Ane looked over at her grandfather. He wasn't coming out from behind the paper anytime soon to help her, but he was still laughing. She then looked behind her mother. She could see something dropping on the floor by the sink. Ane took two steps to the right. As she did, she could see the sink was overflowing? It was overflowing so much that the floor was covered, and so was the draining board. It was almost a sea of red, and it was still moving. Still coming wave after wave.

Ane knew straight away what it was. It was a sea of red gummy bears!

Ane could feel her mother looking at her. She didn't want to look up. She figured she could still look around a little more, and pretend she hadn't seen it. Ane did a 360-spin of the room so her mother knew she had looked at everything. Her mother's glare wasn't going away. Ane opened her big brown eyes as wide as she could and looked up at her mother.

"But, Mum, it was…"

"It was Willow. It is always Willow, Ane. Willow is the best witch in this house. In fact, she may be the best witch in the kingdom."

With that, Willow entered the kitchen. They all stopped to look at her. She looked over at the sink and then back at Ane. With a swish of her tail she walked back out, ran up the stairs, and went back to bed. Willow was sure, even though she did hear her name a few times, that what was happening in the kitchen didn't concern her.

"But, Mum…"

"No buts, Ane. You know the rules. No magic. We only discussed this this morning. This morning, Ane! Your grandfather has had to spend the morning knocking door to door to apologise to all of our neighbours for all the mess you made. He has spent hours putting it all right, hours Ane" Ane's mother paused. Ane was hoping that was the end of it. It wasn't.

"Sorry, I stand corrected for all the mess Willow made… as that was her as well, wasn't it, Ane Maria?"

"But, Mum, it wasn't mess. I was just trying to cut the lawn and then Willow…"

"The lawnmower cuts the lawn, Ane. The reason it has a handle is so that you can push the lawnmower and do your chores. At the weekend. Not on a school day. Not on your own. Not with Magic. Magic does not cut the lawn, Ane."

There was pause. It wasn't a long pause. Long enough for Ane to think of replying, well, actually it can cut the lawn, I proved that, but she knew she was close to a triple-barrelled name at any point now.

"The lawnmower doesn't know the difference between grass, hedges, and flowers, does it, Ane Maria? A magic lawnmower doesn't know the size of our garden, does it, Ane Maria? Seven front gardens. Seven! Totally wiped out. In less than ten minutes. Ten minutes. I don't know how you do it. You amaze even me." At that point Ane's mother flipped her head and looked directly out the window. The third name wasn't coming. It was close, but it wasn't coming. There was almost a laugh at the end of the sentence her mother had said. It was why she had turned away. Ane's mother was trying to keep a straight face at the sight of this morning's gardening escapade. Ane's grandfather lowered the paper to look at Ane and smiled at her, giving her a wink.

"There was no harm done, Lizzy. I put it all back to normal. Better than normal. The Spindleys at number five even paid me to landscape it for them. Asked me to pop back once a month." Ane's mother gave him the look. It was the "don't you defend her" look. No matter how cute

17

she is. Ane had seen her mother give him that look a lot over the last few years. He quickly lifted and hid behind the paper again.

"Ane, no more magic. Do you hear me? I am serious this time."

Ane nodded her head. Her hands had swiftly gone behind her back so that she could cross her fingers, but she was nodding her head in agreement.

"Now, bed with no supper. That is your punishment."

"But, Mum, it just…"

"No 'but Mum'. I swear, sometimes, Ane, they are the only words I ever hear from you. That and 'It was Willow'. No supper, Ane." Ane's mother turned her back and headed over to the sink with her wand in hand to clear up the mess.

Ane headed back out the door towards the stairs.

"Kiss your grandfather before going up."

Ane went back to the kitchen table and jumped up behind the paper to kiss her grandfather. She kissed him on the cheek. As she did he sneaked her a little brown bag which she hid under her cloak and then ran upstairs. As she got back to her room she opened the bag. It was full of red gummy bears. Willow was back, lying on the bottom of her bed. Ane jumped onto the bed and laid backwards, reaching behind her to grab her hat, well, her mother's old hat. It was still about two sizes too big for Ane and it kept falling over her eyes, but she loved it and wore it every day. Especially when she was practising magic. Ane started to eat the red gummy bears. They tasted even better than they had earlier. She figured it must have been because they were clean. Willow came up to the top of the bed next to her and snuggled in for the night.

"We just needed more water, Willow. Then it would have worked."

Willow looked up at Ane and shook her head.

"It will be better next time Willow. Next time it will work."

Chapter 2

"Ane…"

Ane was already halfway down the stairs by the time of the fifth call. Ane always found it hard to get out of bed in time for school.

Saturday and Sunday mornings, she would help her grandfather in the basement with his spells and potions. He would sell them out of town at the weekend markets, and Ane was always allowed to go with him. Saturdays and Sundays Ane would be up at five a.m., dressed and ready to go with no prompting from anyone.

On school days, however, dressing was an effort that took at least thirty minutes. This was after at least three calls from her mother to get out of bed.

"Morning."

Ane's mother was at the sink. Ane's mother always seemed to be at the sink. Her breakfast was laid out on the kitchen table as it always was. Ane walked over and gave her mother a kiss and a cuddle.

"Good morning, my princess. Now go and eat your breakfast… you must be hungry." Ane's mother had counted on the fact that her grandfather would have sneaked her some gummy bears for supper. She also knew that Ane had a secret stash of biscuits and other assorted goodies upstairs in her room. They were in the secret panel at the back of the wardrobe. Along with some drinks and what Ane's mother could only think, were some ingredients for an experiment that sometime in the future she was going to have to clean up.

"Owen will be here soon."

Ane jumped up at the table and started to tuck in to her toast and jam. Owen, her best friend, was always on time. In truth, he was probably Ane's only real friend other than Willow. Owen was an elf. Elves were always known for being brave and courageous. Small, with little pointy ears, and good with a bow and arrow. Owen was small, a couple of inches smaller than Ane anyway. He had shot a bow and arrow once. The arrow travelled almost two feet, twelve feet short of the target, and the three stitches in his right hand took six weeks to heal. As for being brave and courageous, this was something that Owen was yet to grow into.

At school, they shared every class together so they were as thick as thieves. That's what Ane's mother would say to them. Neither of them really knew what it meant. They thought it meant they were in a gang. They both liked the sound of that. Ane's mother liked Owen; he was a good influence on Ane. She knew he was still a little shy and very scared of, well, everything in the kingdom, which was a relief to her. It was what Ane needed in a best friend.

Owen always tried to keep Ane grounded and out of trouble. Tried was a word he used a lot because, however much he tried, they always seemed to get themselves into a little bit of trouble. Normally a little bit too much for Owen's liking.

"Have you finished your school report, Ane?"

"Yes, it is all finished." Ane didn't look up. She just continued to eat her breakfast.

"And you did it all by yourself, Ane? You didn't use any magic, did you?"

Ane knew that was going to be the next question. It was why she didn't look up, for fear of her mother standing over her.

"All by myself. Handwritten and everything." Ane had done it herself. She was careful not, to answer the magic question though.

History was one of her favourite subjects and being asked to write a report on *The Great Book of Everything and Cheese and Onion Sandwiches* was something she really enjoyed doing.

"All by yourself... Owen didn't help you at all then?" Ane's mother knew that as best friends go, Owen was a great one, and she also knew that Ane could pretty much get him to do anything she wanted.

"Yes, he helped a little, but he had his own report to do. His is on King Albert and Queen Sophia so I was only checking we don't say the same things."

Ane finished the last piece of toast as there was a knock on the door. She looked at the clock: 8.16 a.m., exactly the same time every day.

"That will be Owen. Have a good day, princess, and good luck!"

Ane jumped from the table, ran over, and gave her mother another kiss. "You too."

Ane ran to fetch her coat, hat, and her bag and shouted goodbye to her grandfather who she knew would be in the basement. He was always in the basement in the mornings. Well, on the odd occasion he was in the living room, reading, but mainly in the basement. He loved to read, especially the big, thick, heavy types of books. He seemed to have a never-ending supply of books, although when she looked Ane couldn't find them anywhere. It was one of her quests to find his secret library. She knew there was going to be some great spells in there. Owen was at the end of the path leading to Ane's house when she opened the door. He was already looking at his watch.

"We are going to be late."

Ane smiled at him. He said that every morning, and every morning they were five minutes early.

It was about a thirty-minute walk to school. In truth, it was a ten-minute walk to school, but Ane would get distracted at the park, the shops, and sometimes at the stream where they played Pooh sticks on a summer's day, or on a winter's day. Truth be known, most days on the way to school. Owen did know this, and planned it into their walk. He always planned ahead on everything, which, being friends with Ane, was no easy task. Today they were seven minutes early for school, for the first time ever. It was a personal record for them. Owen put this down to how excited Ane was to present to the class on *The Big Book of Everything and Cheese and Onion Sandwiches.*

Owen, on the other hand, was not looking forward to his presentation. He was never comfortable in front of the class. He had researched the royal family from start to finish. He had all the information and knew it off by heart, but he wasn't Ane; he didn't like speaking in public or being the centre of attention. Confidence was something Ane was helping him with. She had even offered him a spell, which he was reluctant to take as yet. Just being close to her gave him more confidence. She gave him confidence that anything was possible because, with Ane, it generally was.

Ane practically skipped into the classroom, and took her seat in the front and centre. It wasn't where she liked to sit, or where she normally sat. Ane had been placed on teacher watch for a week. It was the fourteenth time this year. Accidently turning Sally's hair green was not her fault, Ane was adamant about that... it had been someone else's fault for sure, but she didn't have enough time to think of that other person's name. Willow wasn't at school, and that was the only name she had in her head. So, she was placed on teacher watch. Owen sat next to her. He didn't have to, he wasn't on teacher watch, but he wanted to. Owen sat wherever Ane sat.

The school was huge. It was the only one in the kingdom, and all children attended. Ane's class was always forty-something children strong. It varied slightly, depending which class it was. Not all children attended every class. They weren't all witches. In fact, Ane was the only witch in her year at school. There were a few wizards, a couple of ogres, dwarfs, and elves, although Owen was by far her favourite elf. They even had a giant; his name was James.

Since *The Big Book of Everything and Cheese and Onion Sandwiches,* giants only ever grew to six foot four – but that was still considered to be really tall – there was no need to be any taller, and it meant that giants could live in the kingdom the same way as anyone else.

Everyone came from far and wide to go to school. Anyone who lived on the other side of Horningdale wood or the Sleeping Mountains was allowed to use the Magic Express Way. Anyone who lived further than thirty minutes away from the school was allowed to use it. It was a simple spell that took them from their front door to the school in a matter of seconds through a gateway at the entrance to the school.

Ane had spent three weeks lobbying with the headmistress of the school to let her have access to the Magic Express Way. She even timed herself to school and home again for a month to prove she couldn't make it in thirty minutes. Walking as slowly as she possibly could, her record had been two hours. Unfortunately, her efforts had not worked. The headmistress, Mrs Green, had walked her home one day to prove the point. It took them eight and a half minutes. At that point Ane had decided to change tactics. The very next day, the headmistress had a letter from Ane on her desk asking if she walked the additional twenty-one and a half minutes to one of her classmates' houses, would she then be allowed to use the Magic Express Way? Mrs Green hadn't answered. It had been three weeks. Ane had started penning the next letter, and creating a petition. Ane had made Owen use different coloured pens all week to sign his name, and names of anyone else he could think of, to give it more credibility.

The History lesson wasn't until the afternoon. Ane was going to have to wait to give her presentation. Waiting was never one of her strong points. She spent the whole morning looking at the clock in the classroom, wishing it to go faster.

At lunch, Ane and Owen headed to the history block to give them time to prepare and to be closer to the classroom. This was Ane's favourite place in the whole school. She would often have her lunch and all her other breaks there. She would even stay after school if she could get away with it. She had read all the stories on the hanging tapestries from the days before *The Great Big Book of Everything and Cheese and Onion Sandwiches*, and loved all the fables. Especially the ones about the witches and the wizards taking their rightful place in the world. Owen would always sit there with her. As an elf, the history block held some appeal, although the Elves stories were mostly about war and fighting, which wasn't something he was particularly interested in, he did enjoy the history of magic, though not as much as Ane. Ane loved to talk about The Great Wizards, and Owen loved to talk to Ane. Ane was the main reason he was there. They sat and ate their lunch whilst reading about the greatest wizards in the kingdom for the millionth time. Ane already knew most of it word for word. As soon as the bell rang, Ane almost ran into the class, and sat at the front again, slowly followed by Owen. The rest of the class hustled in behind them one by one.

The class sat noisily waiting for the teacher. Mr Harrison was late. He was always late. Sometimes he was so late that he missed the entire class. Ane was hoping today wasn't one of those days. They had to wait a further ten minutes before he arrived. As always, he was dressed in his long robes, with a long beard, and scraggly hair. Ane always thought he looked like one of The Great Wizards she loved reading about. She would always say he had a wizard's face. He always acted like she imagined a Great Wizard would act too… grumpy!

"Sit down, sit down."

Everybody stopped talking and paid attention. There were rumours around the school that Mr Harrison used to be one of The Great Wizards, one of The Great Six. This meant that most of his students were scared of him. The Great Wizards were the wizards to be scared of. Not for Ane though. Ane wasn't scared. Mainly because it was actually Ane that started the rumours. It had started as an experiment to see how quickly the rumour would get back to her. Owen was the one that actually told Ane about Mr Harrison the day after she started the rumour. She was pleased with that result. It meant that it must have been widely known by then if someone had told Owen. He didn't really have any other friends to talk too.

The rumour never disappeared. It had just grown and grown across the school with other people adding their own piece of the rumour. Now the students stepped out of his path in the corridor. Not that he noticed. Mr

Harrison didn't particularly pay any attention to anyone or anything else around him.

Mr Harrison sat at his desk at the front of the class, and opened his book. He just sat there staring into his book for a further three minutes. He then closed it and dropped the book to the floor, picking up another one from his desk without even looking up to the class. His desk was always full of books. Mr Harrison was known for his books. Ane often thought that Mr Harrison and her grandfather would be good friends because of their love of reading.

Books and carrying his lunchbox with him everywhere he went. That was what Mr Harrison was known for. Ane got off her chair, walked up to his desk, and whispered in his ear. She then returned to her chair. This was something she would do in most lessons. She would remind Mr Harrison what they were supposed to be doing. Sometimes she adapted this so that the class were instructed to do what she liked to do, which had a habit of ending up with Ane on teacher watch again. It took a few minutes but Ane sat still on her chair and waited for him to stop reading.

"Class, we are here for history, history reports. I presume you have all done them? Ane, you go first. Come up here and get on with it." Mr Harrison returned to his book which he had never actually put down.

Ane stood up, pleased with herself, and headed to the front of the class.

Chapter 3

Ane stood up in front of the class, and took out her wand. Immediately the whole class started pushing their chairs backwards towards the back wall of the classroom, leaving Owen in the front row all on his own. Ane knew that Mr Harrison wasn't going to be upset about a little magic. He was a Great Wizard after all. He must have been expecting it, especially from Ane.

She didn't tell her mother she was going to do this either, but as far as Ane was concerned it was just a little visual aid, not real magic. Ane spun the wand around in the air and whispered a spell under her breath. A map of the kingdom appeared above her head. There was a gentle round of applause from the class, some of which was genuine, some of which was out of pure relief. Ane with wand in hand was a scary situation for a lot of them. Most of her class mates had first-hand knowledge of what she could do with a wand.

"In the beginning, there was magic."

The map exploded with fireworks dancing around above her head. Sally was under her desk at this point with her hands on her head, still wearing her hat to hide the colour of her hair. Sally wasn't the only one under their desk. There were a dozen more children in the same position. James the giant even thought about it. He kept looking, but knew he couldn't fit. It had even took Owen back a little, and he had already seen the presentation three times. Ane turned to see Mr Harrison's reaction. The fireworks were a little loud, even Ane thought so. She was very excited and had given them a little more bang than she had in the rehearsal with Owen.

Mr Harrison's head was still in his book; he wasn't paying attention to her. She took that as a sign that she was doing fine. She also thought she could have probably gotten away with more. A good lesson and something she needed to remember for next time.

"In the beginning, there was magic. Magic ruled our kingdom. Wizards and witches were the kings and queens of our history." Ane took a bow at this point. She knew what she said wasn't exactly the truth; the kings and queens of history were, in fact, the kings and queens of history. Wizards certainly had their place though and were important to everyone, but to Ane, the books sometimes didn't give them the credit they deserved. To Ane, wizards and witches were the main attraction of history. Anyway, she figured what was wrong with a little showmanship and imagination? In her mind, she had creative licence to do whatever she needed to do to engage her audience and get top marks in her report.

"The wizards and witches were the real stars that helped shape our kingdom. That was until history gave us the greatest wizard of all time: The Great Burtoni. The

Great Burtoni was the most powerful wizard of his generation and of any generation to come." Ane paused for dramatic effect. It worked. There was another round of applause. She knew she was doing well when some of the children managed to come out from underneath their desks, and just hid behind their chairs.

"The Great Burtoni's power was greater than the rest of The Great Wizards put together. He was feared by all of the kingdom. They feared him even more due to the fact that he never involved himself with the day-to-day life of others." The stories of his greatness were not exaggerated. They actually came from other wizards who had in turn tried and failed to take on The Great Burtoni. They were all secretly quite happy that he didn't care for the politics of the kingdom or the kings and queens. It kept them all in work, and earning gold. Sometimes though, if they ever struggled in negotiations, they would use his name without his consent. The Great Burtoni would have been amazed at the amount of magic he created without knowing about it.

"The Great Burtoni kept himself to himself until one day. One day, looking into the future of our kingdom, The Great Burtoni became concerned. He could only see a future where magic was going to ruin everything that the people had built. The Great Burtoni decided he could not stand idle any more. He knew that he was the only person that could do something about saving our kingdom." Ane had tried to read everything on The Great Burtoni, from his magic to his disappearance nearly one hundred years ago, but there wasn't a lot to read. The Great Burtoni didn't like people very much, and was a very private wizard. As a witch, though, The Great Burtoni was the closest thing to an idol she had known.

"The Great Burtoni realised that The Great Wars were killing our kingdom. The wars, for example, between the forest people and the mountain people were destroying our beautiful landscape. The wars, which had carried on year after year, had ravaged the countryside from the great lake all the way to, well, even here. Here in our little village." Ane waved her wand and a picture of their village appeared above her head.

There was another round of applause. The class was feeling more and more confident in Ane's presentation. Some of the pupils were even moving their chairs forward again.

"The Devil's Dip on the other side of town was actually created by a fireball thrown from the Sleeping Mountains which landed here." Ane pointed to the map. As she did the map swirled around showing the distance from the mountain to the Devils Dip.

"That is a throw of almost thirty miles. A further two and our school would have been part of that dip." Ane was pleased as punch at that fact. Her grandfather had told her that. There was a chance that it wasn't true. Those had been her mother's words, but she trusted her grandfather to be correct when it came to all things related to magic and wizards. He was a great wizard after all. Well, he was the best wizard she knew that lived in the windmill with them, and let her practise magic.

"The Great Burtoni knew deep down that this was all because of magic. The use of magic was making war impossible to live with. Neither wizards nor man had any rules any more. Each of the warring factions would pay a small fortune to be able to secure the skills of The Great Wizards. The Great Wizards, it was said, saved time and lives, but the truth was they actually cost money and cost lives. Not their own lives, but the lives of those who would have to defend their villages and families. A good wizard could wipe out an army while he sat having breakfast..." Ane waved her wand again and silhouettes of all The Great Wizards appeared, walking slowly above her head. This had everyone's attention.

"Fearsome Fred, Disastrous David, The Horrible Hipolito, and The Murderous Manuel. All The Great Wizards had fearful names. Although, if the truth be known, most wizards were just the instruments of the kings and queens. History tells us they just did what they were told. Wizards generally acted out of greed, especially for gold. Gold that they could spend on more materials, which, for them, always meant the creation of more magic. It was always about the magic, and the art of increasing what was possible. For the kings on the other hand, it was all about protecting their lands, they thought other kings wouldn't try to invade if they were protected by a Murderous Manuel or a Fearsome Fred. So, they had to make them sound more ferocious than they actually were." Ane smiled at the class. She knew she had them all in her grasp. Four of the six wizards had already passed above her head.

"Not all of The Great Wizards needed scary names to make them sound invincible though. At least two of The Great Six didn't need them, for two very different reasons." The class at this point knew what was coming. Everyone knew who The Great Six were.

"One of them, The Great Burtoni, because everyone already knew he was the greatest, and the other…" Ane paused again to increase the dramatic effect. This was going better than she had ever expected. The other two wizards appeared above her head. "Was Eric."

The class started to laugh. Everyone loved the story of Eric. He was so popular in the village, they had even dedicated a holiday to him. Every spring they would get two days off school to celebrate the birth of Eric.

"Eric used to be just a normal bunny rabbit who became one of The Great Wizards by mistake. One day, a powerful travelling wizard who had been intending to take part in the great trials of wizardry was practising spells in the forest in front of a mirror. Somehow, accidently, he managed to bounce his own powers off the mirror, and they hit Eric who had just been quietly sitting nearby munching on a carrot. Eric at that moment then became one of The Great Wizards, one of The Six." The class was clapping again.

"The Six were known all over the kingdom to be the greatest wizards in history, but Eric the rabbit was different to the others. He had no interest in war or the state of the kingdom; he was happy spending most of his time being just a normal rabbit. When he did use his powers though, he only used them for good, well, good and the odd giant-sized carrot. That, history tells us, appeared everywhere across the land, even if it was just for a short while." Ane made a giant-sized carrot appear above her head.

Eric was loved by everyone in the kingdom. Every year, parents from all parts of the kingdom would hide carrots in the woods in honour of Eric, and the children would go and find them. Sales of carrots tripled in the spring every year.

There was another figure in the shape of a wizard marching above Ane's head. It was Mr Harrison. She had added a seventh Great Wizard to the list. Some of the class gasped, and then started to whisper to each other about the fact that he was, in fact, a dangerous wizard. There had been some rumours around the class which said he was actually Fearsome Fred in disguise, but Ane knew she didn't need to mention that in her report. The sight of Mr Harrison was enough.

"The Great Burtoni watched as all the other wizards, apart from Eric, gave their skills and services to the kings for hoards of gold. He watched as lives were lost, until he could watch no more. The battles had become something of fairy-tale adventures. If Fearsome Fred had conjured up a fifty-foot dragon to take down the forest people, Disastrous David would conjure up a one-hundred-foot dragon to eat the fifty-foot one.

"Once, the history books tell us, The Horrible Hipolito turned the whole of Manuel's lake army into frogs, and Manuel, in return, tried turning the Horrible Hipolito's mountain people into flies. He was going for flies so that the frogs could eat them for lunch. It seemed like an easy plan. Unfortunately, it wasn't his greatest achievement. For some strange reason, during the spell he had been thinking of his own lunch: Roasted vulture with French fries. The spell was somehow turned around and the flying vultures made light work of his own army. Within thirty minutes it had wiped out half of the mountain people, and the king asked for half his gold back. Magic had no boundaries, and neither did the kings and queens of our lands. The Great Burtoni decided he could watch no more, and he started work to put an end to the madness. He decided he needed to bring rules back to the kingdom."

Ane spoke with such passion that she had the class engrossed in her story. Even Mr Harrison had looked up from his book during the stories of The Great Wizards. She waved her wand above her head again and *The Great Big Book of Everything and Cheese and Onion Sandwiches* appeared above her head.

"The Great Burtoni started to work on restricting the world of magic and creating controls for our great kingdom. He knew the issues were not all to do with magic, but magic had certainly played its part. He began to write the rules that we all now live by."

'Rules' was never a word really used when talking about *The Great Big Book of Everything and Cheese and Onion Sandwiches*. Rules were associated with something that could be broken or changed. Certainly, for Ane they were. *The Great Big Book of Everything and Cheese and Onion Sandwiches* could never be changed, well, not never, but nearly never. There was one way, and only one person who could do it.

"It took The Great Burtoni two years to finish the book, but before he could put his plan into action he needed to find a worthy king. A king fit to rule across all the lands, and who he could entrust with the responsibility of becoming the only person that could change the kingdom The Great Burtoni knew that having one king in charge of everything would help stop the wars."

Ane stopped and looked at Owen. He was already shaking at the thought of standing up and giving his report. They had discussed Owen standing up at this point and quickly saying his report, but deep down she always knew it was never going to happen that way. Owen was shaking his head to remind her just to carry on.

"I know that Owen is going to tell you the full story, but needless to say The Great Burtoni found King Albert's great-great-grandfather, King Albert the Elder. King Albert the Elder wasn't a king at the time, he was a blacksmith. He had fixed The Great Burtoni's horse as he passed through his village. The Great Burtoni judged him to be the most genuine person in the land and decided that he was what all great kings were to be measured against. It is said that Albert wasn't sure he wanted to be king until The Great Burtoni had convinced him that he wanted to be king. The Great Burtoni then took Albert to *The Great Big Book of Everything and Cheese and Onion Sandwiches*."

The book floating above Ane's head now had two figures standing over it: The Great Burtoni and King Albert the Elder. They were both placing their hands on the book.

"Holding Albert's hand to the book, The Great Burtoni sealed the book with a bond, a bond that tied Albert to the book, the book to the kingdom, and both of them to magic. The Great Burtoni was so powerful that as soon as their hands touched the book the spell was cast across the whole kingdom." Ane paused again; it was more to take a breath than for dramatic effect but it got a round of applause none the less.

Everyone knew of *The Great Big Book of Everything and Cheese and Onion Sandwiches*; they knew the story of the book, how it was created, and how it governed the kingdom. The story was taught to all students in Year One of school.

"The Great Burtoni had recreated and secured the kingdom in the creation of one book. A kingdom that had rules, a kingdom that would make a better life for everyone."

There was another round of applause. The class thought that Ane had finished, but when she waved her wand again and the book opened above her head, the clapping stopped.

"It wasn't all plain sailing though."

There was a hush again across the class.

Ane continued,

"One of the key changes that the book brought to the kingdom was that if something wasn't written in the book, if The Great Burtoni hadn't included it, then it no longer existed. Certain things disappeared overnight. They were remembered for a short while by a few, but they no longer had a place in our kingdom."

A picture of a mushroom appeared above Ane's head. There was a gasp as a firework hit the mushroom and it exploded. Her grandfather had told her about mushrooms, fungus that used to grow on the ground that tasted good on toast. It was something that sounded horrible, but that made Ane want to try mushrooms on toast.

"The Great Burtoni had created *The Great Big Book of Everything and Cheese and Onion Sandwiches* to include everything in the kingdom. If it was in the book, then The Great Burtoni had described the meaning of the word and given it rules. For instance, giants like James."

The class turned to look at James. That made James nervous. Ane paying attention to him always worried him. He moved his chair a little bit further back, only a little bit, as he was already at the back of the class.

"Giants like James used to grow twenty-five to thirty feet tall. Now, they only grow to six foot four. The Great Burtoni knew that kings had often used giants in wars, but now, with their new height, they wouldn't be so scary. Now, they could live regular lives like the rest of us."

James tried to smile at Ane. It looked more like a grimace than a smile, but it was the best he could do. He was hoping that she was finished with him now.

The class focused back on Ane. The story known across the land. The Great Burtoni had chosen well in King Albert the Elder. Since that day, peace had continued across the kingdom.

"The Great Burtoni knew the power of *The Great Big Book of Everything and Cheese and Onion Sandwiches*. He knew that in the wrong hands it could be disastrous for the kingdom. For that reason, he made sure that the only person that would ever be able to change the book was now Albert, the blacksmith, and in future years, his family."

Above her head was *The Great Big Book of Everything and Cheese and Onion Sandwiches*, and floating next to it was The Great Pen of Everything. With a swift movement, the book closed, and the pen fell on top of it.

"Wars ended overnight. The kingdom was secure and safe forever."

There was another slight round of applause. Ane loved all the attention. All the kids looked at each other, then at Ane, to see if it was now over. It wasn't.

"There could be no more fairy-tale wars. Magic had been placed into the book. It was now tied to the book forever. Magic, as with everything else, was given rules to live by. No wizard could now intervene with another person. No wizard could go to war. No wizard could cause harm to anyone. These rules gave everyone the greatest gift of all: peace to the kingdom."

There was now a love heart above Ane's head. The class clapped again, and this time Ane took another bow. This made the class clap a little louder; they now knew it was all over. Some of them were clapping because they genuinely liked the story, but most of them were happy they had all survived in one piece.

Ane turned to Mr Harrison who gave her a little nod. He had watched most of the presentation with interest, which was more than she would have ever expected from him. She then ran back to her desk. Mr Harrison returned back to his book and didn't look up again for the rest of the afternoon. Ane had been the only person of interest for him. It was Ane who had then told the rest of the class to get up, one by one, for their presentations.

Ane made Owen go next; she knew he would appreciate getting it over and done with. He got through his presentation the best that he could, although there was a good chance that the snoring noises from Mr Harrison's desk made him lose his stride on a couple of occasions.

That was the excuse he gave Ane anyway.

Chapter 4

King Albert was having his mid-afternoon lunch. He had had lunch earlier and, although it wasn't quite dinner time yet, he was hungry. He was always hungry. Mid-afternoon lunch was a regular thing. He sat in the downstairs kitchen. There was more than one kitchen in the palace. There were seven, but this one was his favourite. This is where cook spent most of her time. He knew he shouldn't be there; Queen Sophia was going to be cross at him for eating in the kitchen. He also knew that this kitchen was where he felt most comfortable. As a king of a kingdom that had no war and no real events to mention, he was a good king. He could handle doing nothing most days. Sophia, on the other hand, had other plans. She wanted to make him into a great king. It didn't matter to her that Albert was happy just being a good king, sitting in the Kitchen having mid-afternoon lunch.

"Sire." Cook came into the kitchen and caught him at the table halfway through a slice of pork pie.

"Sorry, Cook. I was still hungry."

Cook was the only person that spoke to him like a real person. While she always called him sire, she didn't worry what else she said around him. She had been his father and grandfather's cook as well. Albert wasn't sure of her age. She had always been there and she never seemed to get any older. She always looked the same. Exactly how all cooks should look? Happy, and an obvious taster of all the foods she prepared.

"What will the queen say if she catches you down here again, sire?"

"Probably something along the lines of... 'you will ruin your dinner, Albert. Don't eat with the help, Albert. Eat upstairs, Albert. You are a king, you know, Albert, start acting like one.'"

Cook smiled. "You are getting quite good at that impression, sire."

The king laughed. Cook walked over to the side and poured the king a glass of milk to go with the rest of the pork pie. She placed it in front of him.

"Thanks, Cook." King Albert took a big slug of the milk, leaving a milk moustache on his top lip.

Cook just smiled. She couldn't remember a time she thought of the king when he didn't have a milk moustache.

"You know you need to save some room for dinner, sire. We have forty guests this evening."

The king took another slice of pie. "There is always more room for your food, Cook."

It was Cook's turn to laugh at the king. He did always have room. Some days she wondered exactly how much room he had.

"Good, because I have been slaving away all day. They start arriving at five thirty, you know. I am sure these things are getting earlier, sire. Dinner never used to be till eight. You better go upstairs and get all kinged up before the queen notices you are missing, sire."

King Albert was already on his feet at the thought of the queen coming to look for him. He was going to say goodbye as he left, but he still had a mouth full of pie. Cook watched him leave, and then turned back to the stove, laughing to herself.

"Just like his father, and his grandfather... food mad that boy."

***

"Ane, I don't think we should be..." Owen was sitting nervously on the bed. Willow was curled up next to him, watching Ane with interest.

"Don't worry, Owen, it will be fine. I tell you, I nearly had it yesterday. I just needed more water." Ane was busy preparing the same spell as yesterday. At least, she was hoping that was what she was doing. As spells go, Ane always knew the gist of them. Unfortunately, some were too long and took too long to read, so sometimes it was easier to do the short version. She was confident it was practically the same thing when it came to magic.

"But what about the rule? Your mum said..."

"I know what she said, but she doesn't really mean it. Besides, she knows that I can do this spell now; she has seen it in action. Well, almost in action. I think I need to make a few little changes."

Owen was still holding his schoolbooks in front of him. He was almost hiding behind them, as if they could protect him from whatever Ane was about to do. Ane wasn't paying attention to him; she was too focused on the spell.

"I have had another brilliant idea! If we make the gummy bears a little bigger then we can sell them one at a time for more money. We could have a never-ending supply of giant gummy bears."

"Ane, we can't sell six-foot-four gummy bears!" Owen was almost shaking at the thought of it.

"Not giant giants, silly. Just giant compared to the small gummy bears."

Owen didn't say anything more; he knew it was going to go wrong at some point. He also knew that at some point, Ane's mother or grandfather would appear from nowhere and clear it all up; they always did. Ane waved her wand and there was a puff of smoke, but nothing happened. Owen was relieved at that and started to breathe again.

"Ane, maybe if you…"

"No, that's not it, Owen. It has to be the water thing again." Ane ran out of the room and came back with a glass of water. She threw it into her mixture and jumped back as if something was about to spark. Nothing, again.

"I have to go, Ane. It's nearly teatime." Owen was off the bed and heading towards the door before the words registered with Ane.

"Okay, I will see you in the morning. We can have gummy bears for breakfast."

Owen still had thirty minutes before tea, but he was nervous about what was to come. Ane was in "the zone" and that was dangerous for everyone. He gestured to Willow to follow him as he left, but Willow was used to Ane by now. She just lay on the bed still watching Ane.

"Yes, don't be late." With that, Owen was gone, and Ane was back looking at her mixture.

"Maybe it needs to be toilet water, Willow?" Ane disappeared out of the room.

As she did, Willow jumped off of the bed, and left the room. She took one last look at the experiment from the hallway before running downstairs. Willow figured it was probably the right time to take Owen's advice; it would be safer sixty-three steps away, at the bottom of the stairs.

***

"Albert, my love, are you ready?"

"I am just coming, my dear." King Albert was in his dressing room with his butler when he heard his wife, Queen Sophia heading out of the Royal Chamber. He knew she wouldn't wait for him. These functions were more for her than they were for him. He didn't know most of the people that attended. His wife held court better than anyone he knew, and he loved that fact about her. She was a great queen, not just a good queen. She had a magnificent appearance, she was beautiful, a lot taller and thinner than Albert, and always elegant; she was the perfect queen. Her clothes always fitted her perfectly.

Albert always thought that about her. He knew he could have never dreamed of a more perfect wife from the first time they met.

Sophia truly loved Albert too. She loved the fact that he tried his best every day for everyone. King Albert had a kind heart, and she loved him all the more for it.

"Sire, I don't know what to tell you..." The butler continued to try to do up the king's waistcoat.

"I can only presume that it has... shrunk, sire. Yes, I wonder if the wash maiden shrunk it somehow."

The king looked directly at him. His butler's eyes dropped down to the floor.

"That must be it. She has been doing that a lot lately. Someone should really try and train her a little better."

The butler nodded as he took the king's waistcoat off.

"If you give me five minutes, sire, I will sort it out for you." The butler went running from the room. He had become a master sewer over the past few months, and fast. He could let clothes out five inches in less than five minutes. He returned to the dressing room in four minutes and thirty seconds.

"There you go, sire. I just put it in the mangle and stretched it a little, back to its original shape. I will have a word with the wash maiden tomorrow."

The waistcoat went on with ease, and then so did the jacket. King Albert's butler had an afternoon free the previous Tuesday and had taken the opportunity to work on all the king's jackets while he was out hunting. He knew it would save him time, and that awkward conversation around the wash maiden, again. Especially as they didn't have a wash maiden at the palace.

"Thank you, that is perfect. Just a little stretch, you say? Don't be hard on the young girl though, we all have to learn at some point. I am sure she will get there in the end."

The king left the dressing room, and headed to the royal dining room. The butler then took all the king's waistcoats from the wardrobe to the sewing machine. He had a feeling the wash maiden was going to get it right sooner than the king expected.

***

Ane was at the dining table. Hot dogs and hamburgers for tea, covered in lashings of tomato ketchup. It was one of her favourites. Her grandfather was with her, but he was reading the paper again.

"How was school today, Ane?"

"It was good, Mum. My report was great. Everyone gave me a round of applause. Actually, more than one." Ane was very proud of that.

"So I hear, Ane, although I am not sure you needed to go into all of that detail." There was a knowing pause from her mother.

"I heard that the fireworks went down extremely well. Oh, and including Mr Harrison with The Great Six, well, seven now, was a nice touch. Have to keep your rumour mill going, don't you?"

Ane looked up from her dinner at her mother who was still at the sink. There was a snigger coming from behind the paper. Ane's mother always knew everything. No matter what Ane did, she always knew. She turned to face Ane. She was smiling, so she wasn't upset. Ane wanted to ask how, how she knew everything all the time. How Ane couldn't get away with anything at home or at school but in the end, she chose not to continue the conversation. If she knew how, she would always be looking over her shoulder. Besides, it had become commonplace when talking about magic to her mother, to always talk it down a little or gloss over it. So, that is what she did.

"Owen's was good too, Mum. He really knew his stuff. I don't know why he doesn't like getting up in front of everyone. It is so much fun. I love it."

Ane's mother knew what she had done by changing the subject. She just smiled over in Ane's direction.

"So, I hear, dear, so I hear... I think he is still just a little shy."

Ane continued with her tea, but could feel her mum looking at her. The word showmanship was on her lips, to help her explain everything, but she didn't let it escape.

"Now, you know you are staying with your grandfather tonight, don't you, Ane?" Ane's mother walked over to the table where they both sat.

Ane nodded her head with a mouth full of hotdog.

"I am going to the school PTA this evening where I am sure they are only going to say nice things about you,

Ane? What a delightful well-behaved student you are. A real straight A student?"

Ane was nodding her head again.

"Yes, Mum, of course they will."

Ane finished her tea as fast as she could. It was time to depart before her mother said those immortal two words. Ane almost made it to the kitchen door.

"No magic."

Ane pretended not to hear it, and kept going.

"Dad, that means you too."

Ane's grandfather lowered his paper and smiled back at her.

"What is the point? You are both as impossible as each other." Ane's mother went back to the sink. She knew what they would be up to, but she also knew that Ane would be safe with her grandfather. He could clear up any mess that Ane got herself into.

***

King Albert sat at the head of the table next to his wife. She was radiant. She was always so full of life, and loved being the centre of attention. Everyone looked up to her. Unlike Albert, she had always wanted to be queen. Albert was born to be a king, or as he would say, he was made to be a king. Albert watched as they chatted while they all ate dinner. Dinner was his favourite time of the day. Well dinner, breakfast, lunch and second mid-afternoon lunch. Food always came first for Albert. Well, first after Sophia. Food was a close second.

"Excuse me, your Majesty?"

King Albert turned to the person on his right. He had hustled in after running late and hadn't, to this point, noticed who it was sitting next to him. It was a small portly fellow, of very similar build to Albert, with a big bushy moustache, and what clearly looked like a fake beard. He was also wearing an eye patch. Albert looked closely at him. Even with all that, he looked somewhat familiar. He had one of those familiar faces that you have seen a thousand times, but never remembered.

"Yes, sorry, how rude of me. How are you? Are you enjoying your time at the palace?" Albert couldn't stop looking at the beard and the eye patch. They were so obvious.

"It's nice, thank you your Majesty. Your Majesty I was just going to ask if you could pass the mustard."

Albert looked down at the table, he picked up the mustard, put a big dollop on his plate next to his pork pie, and then passed it over to the guest. He looked back down at his plate. It was the fifth piece of pork pie today. Today had been a good day; any day with five pieces of pie was a good day. Albert loved pie.

"Thank you, Your Majesty."

The king turned his attention back to his strange guest who was doing the same thing he had done with the mustard.

"If you don't mind me saying, you look very familiar, sir. Have we had dinner together before?"

"No, Your Majesty. I think I just have one of those faces. People are always saying that to me."

He did have one of those faces… behind the obvious fake orange beard that stood out a mile next to his black moustache, and the unnecessary eye patch that clearly had a hole in it so he could see through it, he had one of those faces that deep down the king knew he should have remembered. One of those faces you would always remember, almost famous. But, as much as he tried, the king just couldn't place him.

"Yes, I guess that's it, you have a very familiar face. Sorry, how impolite of me, what is your name, sir?" The king held out his hand to shake hands with his guest.

"I am the Hor… I mean, Hip… Hip, Hipply, happy to meet you, sire, for the first time of course. My name is… erm… Pedro, yes, erm..Pedro, that is the name. That is my name, Pedro, Pedro."

There was a pause as they both looked at each other.

"Hi… erm… Pedro. Welcome to the palace. Are you sure you have not been here before? Sorry, I am really bad with names and faces." Albert was starting to feel positive that he had seen the man before.

"No, Your Majesty, it's my first time…. Umm, this pie is absolutely lovely. I do love pie."

The change of conversation instantly diverted the king's thought process. Talking about pie was always more interesting. If it was pork pie, even more.

"It really is. Cook is amazing. You know, sometimes she puts an egg in it, right there in the middle. I don't know how she does it, but she does, and it tastes like, like magic."

Erm... Pedro almost choked on the word magic as it came out of the king's mouth.

"It is just lovely, Your Majesty. One of the best I have ever had. Although, I do miss pickle. "

Albert's ears immediately pricked up.

"I am sorry, sir, did you say you missed, pickle?"

***

"Willow, I just don't understand. It worked when you threw it down the toilet. Why not now? Do you think we need to throw it down the toilet? Will that do it? Although I think it is too big now? Do we need to have running water, is that the trick?"

Willow didn't acknowledge Ane. She just lay on the bed licking her paws.

"Something is missing." Ane walked around her spell-making kit, faster and faster, as if the speed was making her think harder. She had watched her grandfather do it many times so it must be the way to get answers.

It wasn't a real spell-making kit, just a couple of beakers and some pipe her grandfather had given her. There was also a funnel she had found in the garden and a shoe. It wasn't just any shoe though. Ane had found it at Devil's Dip and she was convinced that it was all that was left of Fearsome Fred when the fireball hit. For something that wasn't a real spell kit, it had had some surprising results. Ane did credit some of that to the junior spell book her grandfather had given her for her birthday, but some of it was certainly her kit and also some of the magic that she knew was inside her.

"Maybe there is something in the pipes, Willow? Or maybe it is the water in the pipes? Maybe there is something that grandfather put into the water?"

Ane turned and ran down two flights of stairs into the basement, then ran right into her grandfather's study. Her grandfather was sat in his chair, snoring loudly. No matter how much noise Ane made, her grandfather only awoke when he wanted to. Ane had tested this at least a dozen times.

This was a real spell kit. The whole basement was a treasure trove for Ane. She was only allowed in there when she was under supervision. Ane looked over at her grandfather again before heading towards the equipment. She figured having her grandfather there, even if he had his eyes closed, counted as being supervised.

She walked around all of the equipment as if she was seeing it for the first time. The fact was, she was seeing it for the first time as every time she entered the room, it changed. Her grandfather used a decorating spell as a way of creating new ideas. If something didn't work and he needed to see it from another perspective, he would cast a spell and the whole room would change. Ane much to her mother's dismay had inherited her grandfather's genes. He had no patience for magic either, which wasn't a good trait for a witch, and even less for a learning witch. That is why she always had a dozen spells going at any one time.

Her mother would often warn Ane to keep away from the basement, especially when her grandfather was in full flow. She would always threaten her that there was a risk that one day she would end up as wallpaper during one of his spells.

Although everything in the room changed often, there was one thing that was a constant in her grandfather's basement: his old battered trunk, his magic trunk. That was where her grandfather kept everything important, everything that he wanted to keep safe. On the top of the trunk was a number lock. An eight-digit number lock. It was always set at 00000000. Ane always wondered what this was for as it had padlock loops as well, there was surely no need for both? Although the padlocks were never placed on the trunk. It would always just open. Her grandfather never spoke to Ane about the numbers, so she figured they couldn't be that important. He often spoke about the trunk, but not the numbers.

He would tell Ane how through The Great Wizards' wars, they would all climb in there and be safe. Apparently, it was bigger on the inside than it looked. Ane had never tested that theory. She had thought about it, but had never actually done it. She almost managed to get Willow to jump in once by leaving treats all the way down to the basement leading to the open trunk. Willow had eaten most of the treats, but had been just too clever to fall for it.

Ane's grandfather told her that the trunk was protected with the most powerful magic in the kingdom; nothing could harm you once you were inside. She was ninety percent sure that was true. Although it did sound like another one of the stories her mum said were just stories.

There was another story about the trunk that interested Ane more, one her mother wouldn't let her grandfather tell her. It involved eight wizards. He had started the story one Saturday evening, returning from a night at the local tavern. Ane had been reading about The Six, when her grandfather had told her there weren't only six. Ane's mother stopped the story dead as soon as she realised what he was talking about. Ane had never seen her mum so cross with him. Ane pushed and pushed her grandfather when they were alone again, but he was under orders not to tell her.

Ane always believed her grandfather's stories. He was the most amazing man she knew. It didn't matter that the stories made him over one hundred and seventy years old. She just figured that was probably his real age. Her mother, on the other hand, would always say that some of them were just stories. Ane knew that she only did that to try to make her obey the rules, just in case he slipped up and told her the odd spell. Which he did quite often, on purpose.

Ane never dared to get in the trunk though; she was convinced that her grandfather had deeper, darker secrets inside there. While magic couldn't hurt you in there, her grandfather had also told her that magic couldn't get out either. Which made her worry what type of magic was in there. For some reason, he religiously kept his wand in the trunk when it wasn't in his hand. That had always intrigued Ane. She checked – it wasn't in his hand now. Maybe that is what the trick needed, just a little wave of her grandfather's wand. He wouldn't mind; he was basically supervising her when she took it.

Ane walked over, and stood in front of the trunk. She looked back at her grandfather, who was still snoring, before placing her hands on the lid. Slowly she started opening it with shaking hands.

"BOO!"

Ane nearly jumped out of her skin. Fortunately, she knew her grandfather's voice or she wouldn't have doubted she would have been running up the stairs screaming. He was laughing as the lid went back down with a thump.

"What are you looking for in there, young lady?"

"Nothing. I was just…"

"Nothing, eh? You weren't looking for a little magic in my trunk? Perhaps to help with a spell or two that you are working on upstairs?"

Ane started to laugh too.

"No, not me. No magic that is the rule. You heard what Mum said." Ane ran over and hugged her grandfather.

"Grandfather, I only came to ask you a question. Is there anything in the pipes in this house? In the water pipes, I mean?"

Ane's grandfather lifted her on to his knee. "What do you mean, in the water, Ane?" He knew what Ane meant. It didn't take him long to figure out that water and magic equals yesterday's sea of gummy bears spell was being worked on again in Ane's room. He also knew she wouldn't give in that easily.

"Like, erm, magic?"

He pondered for a moment, as if trying to remember something for Ane.

"Now, there is a question. This is a magic house, Ane, I have been known to do the odd piece of magic, and so has your mother. Not you though, because you are a good girl." Her grandfather was laughing as he was talking.

Ane was nodding her head.

"I think there is a good chance that magic can leak down a drain or escape from a broken beaker. I guess, you never know where it might end up."

Ane was smiling the biggest smile. She loved the thought that magic was everywhere.

"Why do you ask, young lady?" He knew why Ane was asking, but he also knew he wasn't going to get an answer. Nevertheless, it was fun to ask.

"No reason." Ane jumped up, gave him a kiss on the cheek, and ran back upstairs.

Her grandfather went over to the trunk, and took out his wand. Something told him he was going to be needing it shortly.

Chapter 5

"Pickle? Did you say pickle?" King Albert had never heard that word before, but there was something about it that rolled off his tongue.

"Yes, sire, pickle. I..." Erm... Pedro stopped mid-conversation again and looked closely at the king. Anyone else would have seen he was just checking if he had the king's full interest, but Albert was so engaged in the conversation he didn't even notice.

"I mean... well, it's just something my grandfather used to say. He used to say that there was always pickle with pork pie. He never had pie without it. Or cheese, come to think of it."

Even behind the fake orange beard, the big bushy moustache, and the fake eye patch, you could tell that the man called Erm... Pedro was smiling. The king had taken the bait.

"Pickle, pickle! What an odd little word." Albert was rolling the word around on his tongue as if he was actually eating the pickle.

"Do you know what it was? It sounds delightful." Erm... Pedro smiled at the king.

"I believe it was some sort of condiment, sire. Spicy and sweet at the same time. Sugar and spice and all things nice, my grandmother used to say. Better than that boring old mustard – that was another thing she used to say."

Albert looked down at his mustard. As long as he could remember, there was only ever mustard. There was no alternative.

"Sweet and spicy at the same time you say? At the same time..." Albert went back to his food, but suddenly pickle was all he could think about. It sounded like something you would want if you were a king, something you deserved as a king. Yes, it sounded like something that would go great with his pie. His normal old pie, the pie he had to eat five times today with boring old mustard, and no, no pickle.

Erm... Pedro watched intensely through the hole in his eye patch as the king looked around the room at everyone having their pie with mustard.

"Although, sire, come to think of it, it was no sausage and peanut butter sandwich. Well, that's what he used to say, Your Majesty."

Albert was holding his normal old pork pie at the time, and dropped it on the floor.

***

"Willow, I have decided, I think we need to think about flushing the experiment."

Ane was back in her room. After speaking with her grandfather, she was now convinced that the water pipes had something in them. Probably something that disappeared when it came out of the tap so she never drank it. Her mother would have made sure of that. This gave Ane another idea. She started to wonder how she could bottle magic water and sell it at school. It would be good for her friends. Well, mainly for one friend, maybe it would give him some confidence. Ane could tell that Willow wasn't too convinced with the flushing plan. To be fair Willow didn't really care either way; she was more interested in the mouse she thought she had seen running across the stairs.

"But if we do this Willow, they won't fit out of the tap. In fact, I am sure he wouldn't even fit down the toilet, we have made him too big! Umm, maybe we need a spell that will make a bigger tap?"

Ane was standing looking at the prototype they had made. It was a big gummy bear. They were never going to make it reproduce down the tap. Ane jumped back onto the bed, grabbed Willow and started to stroke her.

"Come on, Willow, we need a plan."

Willow wiggled out of Ane's arms, jumped off the bed, and headed over to her bed on the floor. She had a better angle of the stairs from there to see the suspected mouse that had invaded her house. Willow didn't need to get caught up with Ane's plan. It didn't mean she wouldn't help her with an idea though. As she headed to her bed, she stopped and rubbed herself up against the laundry hamper while looking directly back at Ane. Willow did it again. Ane didn't seem to be getting the hint. Willow rubbed herself against the hamper once more.

"Laundry, Willow? What about the laundry?"

Willow took ten paces back, ran at the basket, and knocked it over. She then returned her stare back to Ane.

"Willow?"

Willow walked over to the laundry basket, picked up a piece of washing, took it to the bedroom door, and dropped it.

"You want me to put the washing machine on? Willow, concentrate, we are coming up with a spell! Mum will do the washing. We need running water for the gummy bear. I just said it won't fit out of the tap. Where else can we get running water?"

Willow went back to her bed and cuddled up with a smile on her face. Keeping one eye secretly on the stairs.

It took Ane almost a minute to come up with the brilliant idea that Willow had clearly put into her head.

***

"Excuse me? Sausage and peanut butter? Did you say sausage and peanut butter?"

"Yes. You know, Your Majesty, when the hot sausage melts into the peanut butter, and makes it all sticky... There is nothing better."

Albert had never drooled this much. The thought had his mind ticking over at a hundred miles an hour.

"Well, that's what my grandfather used to say, sire. Wise man my grandfather."

Albert sat back in his chair. He suddenly had an urge to meet Erm... Pedro's grandfather.

"But sandwich? You know, sandwich, as in, the sandwich?"

"Yes, sire. As in the sandwich?"

"And, it was sausages with butter and some peanuts?"

"I know, it sounds strange, doesn't it? You know how grandfathers are, Your Majesty, all full of stories. He said it was the best sandwich he had ever had... Grandfathers eh? I mean, who ever heard of a knickerbocker glory? Ice cream, chocolate sweets, and sauce, lots of sauce. All together in the same glass? He said it was like eating a small piece of heaven. Silly old grandfather. Always full of stories."

Albert was now completely lost in the world of his new best friend, Erm...Pedro, and what he could only think was a great wizard of a grandfather.

***

Ane carried the gummy bear down the stairs and into the kitchen. Well, it wasn't so much of a carry as the bear bumped on every step. Her grandfather could hear her from the basement. He was smiling to himself; he knew she was up to something. Knowing Ane though, he also knew he had some time. He was working on an experiment of his own: an automatic lawnmower that knew the boundaries of the garden. Ane's previous little experiment had given him the idea, and getting paid for landscaping had given him the incentive. He was sure though he was looking at the situation from the wrong angle... maybe he needed a little redecorating experiment of his own.

***

The dinner was coming to a close, and the king's new best friend had disappeared like most of the other guests. The queen was saying her final goodbyes. Albert was fully engrossed in the table of food that was laid in front of them. There was still loads left. This would normally be his favourite sight and favourite time of the night... leftovers. Now, he was seeing it through different eyes. It had been the same table of food every night. Every night since he could remember, there was never anything new. There was never going to be anything new. Never going to be pickle or peanut butter.

The king's mind had started to wander to all the new wondrous stories that he had heard. The wondrous foods he had heard about in particular. Erm... Pedro had spent the rest of the evening talking about exciting food that his grandfather had told him about. Food that the king had never heard of before.

"Are you coming to bed, my dear?" The queen had seen the last guest out.

"Shortly, my dear."

The queen gracefully walked over and kissed the king on the cheek before disappearing into the palace. She was sure he was about to have a second, maybe third, dinner in her absence. The king continued to stare at the table of remains.

"Knickerbocker glory, that is what he said, and pickle? Pickle, I wonder if you can put pickle on a knickerbocker glory." The king was speaking out loud. Nobody in the palace could hear him… or so he thought!

***

Ane dragged the gummy bear into the kitchen and up to the washing machine. She opened the door, looked inside, and then looked back at the gummy bear. She squeezed the gummy bear into the machine and leaned up against the door until she managed to close it.

"I knew it would fit, Willow!" Ane pulled a chair up to the cupboards. She climbed onto it, opened the cupboard doors, and then started to look inside.

"What do you wash a gummy bear in, Willow?" Ane stood looking at the jars all lined up in the cupboards. She made up her mind.

"Honey, sugar and… jam. I think that will do it." Ane grabbed them, went back to the washing machine, and started filling it with her concoction.

Willow remained by the door of the kitchen, far back, enough to be safe, but close enough to see her actual plan fall into place.

Ane switched on the machine.

***

King Albert was troubled. He had always been told that *The Great Big Book of Everything and Cheese and Onion Sandwiches* was only to be opened in a time of great need. His grandfather and father had constantly repeated that to him. His grandfather had told him that The Great Burtoni himself had told him to never change anything. Never change anything unless it was a matter of life or death, never!

Albert, as king, was now the only one with this power. He could open and change the book. It could only be done by his hand. As a descendent of Albert the Elder, he, and he alone, had the ability to make the world a better place.

Albert was becoming more and more convinced that the world would be a better place with knickerbockerglory's, sausage and peanut butter sandwiches... and pickle, sweet and spicy at the same time, pickle.

Albert knew it wasn't exactly a life or death situation, but if he did this, he would be doing it for his fellow man; for his kingdom. Change would be good for the kingdom.

His people would love him for it. This would make him a Great King, and Sophia would love the fact that he had, at last, become a Great King. That must be a good thing. The king stood up and headed for The Great Hall of Books.

***

"Willow, I am not sure how long the washing machine takes."

The washing machine had started to whir, which in itself was a change. The washing machine never normally made a noise; it was silent. But today, today, it had started to whir.

"Maybe I should...?" Ane took out her wand and walked over to the machine. It was still a training wand. She knew it was a training wand, a low-level wand for children under ten years old. It wasn't going to do that much damage.

Ane constantly argued with her mother that, given she had the intelligence of a twelve-year-old, she should have been upgraded by now. To this day, her mother hadn't given in.

She tapped the wand on the washing machine, and it stopped whirring. She went back and sat on the chair in front of it. It had stopped whirring; it was more a clunking sound now. She turned to look at Willow who had moved a little further back into the hallway.

***

In The Great Hall of Books there were many, many books. In fact, most of the books in the kingdom were found there. When The Great Burtoni cast his spell across the kingdom, the things that he had forgotten to put into the book disappeared. They simply no longer existed. People, over time, had forgotten about most of the actual things themselves, but they couldn't forget about the books. If it disappeared in the real world, it did in the literary world too. So, the books had more holes now than Swiss cheese. Some books had words missing from every line, which made them unreadable. Over time, they found themselves being placed in The Great Hall of Books as they needed to go somewhere.

The Great Burtoni had realised sometime after writing the book that there were a lot of things he didn't know about his kingdom. Being involved in the day-to-day life had never been his forte, which meant that a lot of things he didn't know about had disappeared overnight. He should have probably kept up with everything and written a second book, but that would have required him to do more research, something he never quite got around to doing.

In the centre of the room stood *The Great Big Book of Everything and Cheese and Onion Sandwiches* on its own pedestal. The king would let visitors view the book on a daily basis, especially schools and history classes. He loved to hear the story as much as they did about how his grandfather had become king and saved the kingdom from itself.

King Albert stood in front of the book. He had never used it before. In fact, his father had never used it before and neither had his father before him. Albert was convincing himself that change was good. He really believed that change was good, especially today. He placed his hand on the front of the book, and as he did so, the book started to glow and open in front of him.

Albert's eyes lit up. He had never even opened it before, it was amazing!

"Wow!" The king held his breath as he watched the book glow brighter and brighter.

"Wow, indeed," a voice echoed behind him.

The king instantly turned to see where the voice had come from. He was sure he was alone in there. Before he had time to see anyone though, he realised that he was starting to lift off the ground. He was floating away from what was now the "open" *Great Big Book of Everything and Cheese and Onion Sandwiches*.

***

The washing machine had stopped after dancing around for the last fifteen minutes… side to side, up and down! It had shaken so much Ane was surprised it hadn't danced its way out of the kitchen. Willow was now on the first step of the stairs, peering around the corner. She could just about make out Ane and the washing machine. Ane walked over to the washing machine and opened the door… nothing happened. She could see the red gummy bear all squashed up, but it looked the same. It was still red and soft-looking. She half-expected it at least to have shrunk a little. She gave it a poke to see if it felt the same.

"Ouch!"

Ane jumped back. It sounded like the gummy bear said ouch. She turned around to see if her grandfather was behind her throwing his voice. He wasn't. She then looked for Willow. She was nowhere to be seen. She looked back at the washing machine and started to see some movement. The gummy bear was wriggling around to see if it could get out. With a POP! the gummy bear stood in front of Ane. Ane froze.

"Hello."

Ane didn't answer. For the first time, she was stuck for words. In front of her was a real-life talking gummy bear. Something had gone wrong. She wanted everlasting gummy bears to eat. The gummy bear walked over to the table and hopped up on a chair.

"What's for tea? I think, I am hungry?"

Willow's head popped around the corner. She was intrigued by the silence that followed after the washing machine had stopped, and now the strange voice coming from the kitchen.

"Umm, I am not sure? What do gummy bears eat?"

The gummy bear looked over at the cupboard.

"I am not sure either? I have never eaten anything before?"

Ane was walking over towards the gummy bear sitting at her kitchen table.

"How about some honey? I like honey, and I think there is another jar."

The gummy bear nodded. Ane was smiling now. Sure, the experiment had gone a little wrong, but now she had a real-life gummy bear in her kitchen. She jumped back on the chair and started looking through the cupboard.

"I am Ane, by the way. And you are?" Ane looked at the gummy bear.

He shook his head. It was more of a wobble than a shake.

"Oh, you don't have a name. I think we will call you George. What do you think Willow? George is a good name." Willow heard her name but she didn't respond.

"George." The gummy bear repeated his name. He was smiling.

"It is a good name, George."

Ane found the honey. She turned to show her new best friend. As she did she heard a... POP! Ane dropped the jar on the floor and it smashed into a thousand pieces.

***

"Erm... Pedro?" The king was now floating five feet above the book.

"Mwah, mwah, mwah... yes, it is I, the master of disguise, Erm...Pedro." Erm... Pedro grabbed hold of his false beard and his eye patch, ripped them off, and threw them across the room.

"Or should I say... it is I... The Greatest Wizard of all the kingdom!" Erm... Pedro had his arms lifted in the air as if beckoning the king to worship at his feet, well, from five feet above the ground.

"I knew I knew your face. You... you are The Great Burtoni?"

Erm... Pedro's arms went straight down by his side with a THUD! There was a frown on his face now.

"NO! No, it's me, The Horrible Hipolito! Feared across the whole kingdom, the bringer of the..."

"Frogs?"

"No... not the bringer of the frogs. That wasn't the plan. Why do people only ever remember the frogs?"

There was a moment of silence, as if The Horrible Hipolito was sulking. He didn't sulk for long.

"The bringer of the dragons! The bringer of the magic! The bringer of the thunder!" The Horrible Hipolito gave a thunderous bad guy laugh. He had had the same laugh for the last two hundred years. He had perfected it to see if it scared the other wizards away. It didn't. Wizards didn't really get scared, although the laugh certainly was loud and thunderous.

The king could see it now, the face that he knew he had recognised during dinner, the face behind the obvious disguise. He couldn't believe it had not struck him sooner. There were pictures of The Great Six everywhere in The Great Hall of Books.

"But, that is not possible? You are... you should be...?"

"I am what? Dead? I bet that is what everyone in the kingdom thought? I bet they thought we had all died out. Well, it is not true! It's all his fault. You should know Wizards only die if they want to. Or, if they get lazy, and forget to carry on living. Believe me that has happened more than once. No, this was his fault! Our absence was thanks to The Great Burtoni, and his magic book. I sense we will find he had some small spell written in the book somewhere which took us all by surprise. Something that says that you will be frozen for one hundred years if you were to use magic to interfere with life. That's what happened to us... to all of us!" The Horrible Hipolito gave a shudder as if remembering what it had been like to be frozen for one hundred years, especially frozen for one hundred years next to Fearsome Fred. That wasn't a sight you wanted for one hundred years, or a smell. Even through the ice you could smell him.

"Do you know what it's like to be frozen for one hundred years? No? It is cold, I can tell you that, cold and very boring. Especially when I needed a pee just before... grhhh, stupid spell!"

The king watched as The Horrible Hipolito started to look through *The Great Big Book of Everything and Cheese and Onion Sandwiches*.

"You know you can't change anything in the book; I am the only one that can use The Great Pen of Everything, and I will not help you. I just simply won't." The king sounded quite pleased with himself with that comment.

"I know that. I also know The Great Burtoni. The second greatest wizard of all time. Always struggled to name anything. *The Great Book of Everything...* The Great Pen of Everything, I mean, did he sit on The Great Chair of Everything? Eat from The Great Plate of Everything? He never did have an imagination. That's why we didn't let him play with us – no imagination."

The king didn't answer. He was a Great Burtoni fan. Under his influence, war had finally ceased, and at last the kingdom was united. It is why he was the only wizard with "Great" before his name. That must have counted for something.

"Besides, I don't need The Great Pen of Everything, I wasn't looking to change the book. It took us a while to figure out what he had done. Thanks to him, we had one hundred years to figure it out though." The smell of Fearsome Fred was still in his nose. Every time he sniffed, he could smell him, and every time it brought back the memories of the last one hundred years, and how much he didn't like The Great Burtoni.

"See, we figured that given The Great Burtoni's attention span... you know him, always with his head stuck in a book somewhere, but never for long..." The Horrible Hipolito stopped flicking through the book; he had reached the page he liked. The king watched as The Horrible Hipolito's smile got bigger and bigger.

"Given his attention span, we all knew what he would have done, and it would seem we were correct" The Horrible Hipolito picked up the book and turned it. "He was always up for a shortcut. You see, he bound the book page by page as he was only able to write one page at a time. That's why it took him two years, during which we knew he was up to something, we just didn't know what. He then bound the book to the kingdom, so all I need to do is..."

***

Pop! Pop! Pop! It wasn't stopping... Pop! There was another one, then another, and then another gummy bear... alive in the kitchen.

After the second one appeared, Ane had looked at George, preparing herself to come up with another name, but before either of them could say anything, there was a third and a fourth. Ane counted to thirty before really starting to panic. Thirty was certainly going to get her mother to use all three of her names. Thirty quickly turned into forty, and Ane started having visions of the sink the previous night. The overflowing red sea of gummy bears was now a red sea of giant red gummy bears.

"Is this supposed to happen?"

George was still sitting at the table, waiting for some honey. Ane was frozen on the chair as the other gummy bears started to run amok across the kitchen. They were now leaking into the hallway and across in the living room. Ane was sure she heard the front door open. Yes, this was definitely going to be a three-barrelled name telling-off.

***

"As I was saying, all I have to do is… now, where did I put those scissors?" The Horrible Hipolito started to look through his robes.

Albert was sure he wasn't wearing robes at dinner. He would have definitely known he was a wizard if he was wearing robes, he was sure of that. He thought again, he couldn't be totally sure he would have noticed; he was side tracked by the talk of food. The talk of all that glorious food, glorious food…

"The knickerbockerglory? Pickle? Was any of it really real?" Now it was the king who was trying to distract him in the hope that someone else would find them. That, and the king deep down really wanted to know if any of the foods they discussed were real. If he was honest to himself it was more for the second reason. He knew that if they were discovered, nobody else was going to be able to do anything to stop him. The Horrible Hipolito was a wizard, and while wizards had rules, he was still a wizard.

"Mwah, mwah, mwah." He didn't need to do the laugh, but it had been a hundred years since he had been able to use it, so he was determined to take as many opportunities to use it as he could.

"I knew that was the way to get you to open the book. One look at you and I knew. All I had to do was plant the seed. Plant the seed, and then wait for you to start thinking about food. Just so you know though, they were actually all real. There were a lot of great foods in this world before..." The Horrible Hipolito folded the book back on itself to read the title.

"Before *The Great Big Book of Everything and Cheese and Onion Sandwiches*, you will be pleased to know.... Wait, why is it called *The Great Big Book of Everything and Cheese and Onion Sandwiches*? How stupid is that?" The Horrible Hipolito looked up at the king.

The king shrugged his shoulders. He had asked the same question before. Actually, everyone in the kingdom had asked the same question before.

"What a stupid name. Okay, where was I? Oh, yes, there were a lot of things in this kingdom before this book… pineapple… I haven't seen a pineapple. I bet he forgot about them too. They were great on pizza. Pizza, I don't remember the last time I saw a pizza. You will be pleased to know there will be a lot of great things again in our kingdom. Now, where did I put those scissors?"

***

The popping was getting louder and more frequent. Ane tried to keep count in her head, but she lost the number after it got to the hundreds, maybe thousands. For a brief second, Ane did wonder whether she should get them to sign her petition – her teacher would not be able to discard so many signatures – but it was only a brief second.

It sounded like popcorn exploding on the stove. That was at the forefront of Ane's mind. The washing machine exploding, and gummy bears pouring out of everywhere. Ane's experiment was now up the stairs, in the living room, running havoc all over the house, and even out in the street.

"Come on, George." Ane grabbed Willow from the bottom step, and headed down to the basement.

When she arrived, the room was in mid transformation. Everything was spinning around, glasses, bottles, and furniture, all floating in the air. It looked like they were in the middle of a hurricane. The only constant was the trunk in the middle of the room. It was stood perfectly still; magic had no effect on it. She was scanning the room looking for her grandfather. He was there in the corner of the room. He was mid spell. She could tell from his eyes; they were glazed over and white. She knew the rules: you never interrupt a wizard mid spell, anything could happen. She didn't think twice. She knew what she had to do; it was her only option, no matter how scary it was.

She stood in front of the trunk. All the number digits were set at zero. 00000000. It must be open. She lifted the lid, and opened the trunk. It looked fine. It looked empty. There was just one wand at the bottom of the trunk. Ane jumped in with Willow. George jumped in too before the lid closed. Ane could hear the room transforming, and in the distance, there was still a faint sound of something that now sounded like a machine gun. POP! POP! POP!

***

"Here they are! Now, all I need to do, your Majesty, is…" The Horrible Hipolito snipped at the binding of the book and then pulled out a page. "BOOM!"

There was a noise; a loud noise. It shook The Great Hall of Books so much that books started to fall from the shelves. The books were opening as they fell, and the king could see they were rewriting themselves. The missing words that had disappeared one hundred years ago had started to appear, right there on the page. The king had no idea but this was happening all across the land. The things and places that had been forgotten were returning.

"Snip the binder! You didn't protect that, did you, The Great Burtoni? All I had to do is pull the thread and take the page with magic written on it out of the book. Thanks to The Great Burtoni protecting each sheet separately, magic will still be in the kingdom, but the kingdom will no longer be ruled by it. When I say magic will be still be in the Kingdom you understand nobody has magic now, only I do!" The Horrible Hipolito paused. Even the king knew what was coming next.

"Mwah, mwah, mwah."

The king gave a little smile. It felt rude not to.

"The book has no magic. You see, the magic in the kingdom was bound to the book and the page was bound to the book. Without the page the book and the kingdom have nothing. But I have everything. So, Your Majesty, now you can eat all the sausage and peanut butter sandwiches you like."

The king was still engrossed with the books. They were flying everywhere. With every returning word, the book shot off in a different direction. It was like watching fireworks. The Horrible Hipolito was engrossed with the page he had in his hands. It still had the rules on it though. While he was the only one with magic, the rules still applied. They were protected on the sheet. The last one hundred years hadn't given him an answer to that part... Not yet! But he knew the Great Burtoni there was going to be a way to break the rules.

"Now, Your Majesty, I am back to being the one, the only, the most powerful wizard in the kingdom."

"I thought you said you already were the most powerful wizard in the kingdom?"

"I am! I am the most powerful. What I meant to say was that now I am the only person that has magic... so there." The Horrible Hipolito smiled and placed the page in his top pocket.

"But there are rules! There are still rules; bound to that page," The king wasn't sure if there were still rules, but he really hoped there was or else he was going to be in trouble. Well, more trouble than the trouble he was already in.

"There is, Your Majesty, but I have a plan for those too. Rules are made to be broken, Your Majesty."

The Horrible Hipolito waved his wand and the king fell to the ground with a thud. The Horrible Hipolito then waved his wand in the air and gave a big clap. He looked around. He remained exactly where he was.

"Still, still no transportation... still I have to walk! What kind of exit is that for the greatest wizard of all time? I really miss the old days." The Horrible Hipolito tried to walk backwards and quickly to exit the Great Hall of Books. He was trying to make himself look mysterious as he did, but ended up bumping into the bookshelves, twice.

The king gave a little laugh under his breath, not a big laugh as he still wasn't sure how much damage the wizard could do if he wanted to. The king stood up, dusted himself down, and walked over to *The Great Big Book of Everything and Cheese and Onion Sandwiches.*

He opened the book. Nothing happened... no glow... nothing. It was now just a book, a book of words. Not even a book with all the words any more. At least one he knew of was missing. That word was Magic.

Chapter 6

There was a massive crash. Ane felt as if the house had come down around the trunk. She didn't want to move. She had a vision of the house collapsing under a million gummy bears, and she was going to have to eat her way out. That would take hours, maybe even days. Then she remembered that they might all be alive. She wasn't going to be able to eat a living gummy bear. She couldn't eat George, he was her friend now. That wasn't going to work. She was going to have to give them all names, and then, maybe they would just sort of blend in. Ane gave it five minutes before daring to push the lid open. When she did, the first thing she could see was her grandfather. He was sat in his chair. He looked exhausted, well, he was at least breathing hard. She climbed out slowly, followed by Willow and George. Ane walked over to her grandfather's chair.

"Sorry." Ane was looking directly at her grandfather.

He didn't answer. She figured it was because he had not heard her. She was trying her hardest to be cute and small, but she was going to have to say a real sorry this time. One he could hear.

"Sorry, Grandfather."

He looked down at her. She had used her best "It wasn't my fault voice" but even she knew that might not work now. Not even on her grandfather.

"Sorry, Ane? What for?"

Ane looked around the room, and then looked back at her grandfather. She didn't have to point out all of the mess; it was obvious. There were smashed beakers and bottles everywhere. The room looked like it had been twisted and then frozen in time. The chairs and tables were there, but they were sort of stretched... one chair must have been at least ten feet long. Ane was also checking the room for something else, anything red, but she couldn't see any. Other than George, there was not another gummy bear in sight. Ane let out a sigh of relief, then she glanced, cutely, up at her grandfather. This had to be her fault somehow. Although she wasn't sure how the gummy bears would have stretched the chair.

"Oh, Ane, this has nothing to do with you! Something has gone seriously wrong. The spell just stopped in mid flow. I don't understand. This has never happened to me before."

Ane was looking directly at him now. He looked worried, He looked very worried. She looked around the room again. She could see what he meant, the room had stopped mid spin. Ane tried to think how the gummy bears had managed that. Her grandfather stood up. He tried to start the spell again. Nothing happened. Nothing changed. Ane had never seen her grandfather fail at magic before. For her, he was magic.

"Maybe…" Ane's grandfather went over to his trunk. His wand was still in there. He didn't need it to do a quick transformation spell. This was something he did daily. He took out his wand and recited a quick "tidy up" spell… nothing! He pointed the wand at the entire room, and said it again. Still nothing. Something appeared on her grandfather's face; something that said the situation was serious. He couldn't make his wand work. The wand had magic. It was born out of magic. But it needed someone with magic to be able to direct it. Now, it wasn't working.

"There is something wrong with my magic, Ane! It doesn't seem to be working? None of it…" Her grandfather looked really worried now, and a little sad.

Ane walked up to him and gave him a big hug. It was all she could think to do.

"Maybe it is just having a rest? It could be tired?" Ane tried to comfort her grandfather, but she had never seen him looking this sad.

There was a long pause as her grandfather looked around the room. Ane hugged him again which seemed to bring him out of whatever he was thinking about.

"Maybe, maybe that is all that it is, Ane." He smiled down at his granddaughter.

"But let's not worry about that now. Let's get you to bed. It must be nearly bedtime."

As he picked Ane up, she gave him a kiss and another cuddle. He started to carry Ane up the stairs.

"You are getting so heavy, Ane. You weigh a tonne." He pretended to struggle carrying her up the stairs which made her laugh. Just a short laugh though, as Ane was suddenly aware that they were going upstairs. She needed to think fast. She needed a reason for what had happened upstairs. She was going to have to explain why the house was full of red gummy bears, and what they had done to their furniture... Ane was starting to feel worried about the discovery that her and her grandfather were about to make.

"Grandfather..."

"Yes, Ane?"

Ane was listening as hard as she could, but she couldn't hear the popping anymore. She was sure it had stopped.

"Well, Willow and I, but mainly Willow... I was just helping her, we were just—"

"What has happened to my lovely house!"

As Ane's grandfather pushed open the door to the basement Ane could hear her mother coming through the front door. She was sure there was going to be a three-barrelled name call following the words her mother had just said.

"I was going to stop her, but..." Ane was ready with her response. She was using her sweet and innocent voice again, but nobody heard her above the still crashing sounds from around the house. Ane looked everywhere for the colour red, she couldn't see a gummy bear anywhere, well, other than George, who was hiding behind her grandfather's legs at that moment.

"I am sorry, dear, I think it must have been me. Something has happened downstairs. My magic stopped… The transformation spell stopped in mid flow. I am guessing when it did, it shook the whole house."

Ane's mother was shaking her head in disappointment. She stopped when she saw the look on his face. Something told her this was more serious than it sounded.

"The thing is, I can't even do a simple clean-up spell now."

Ane looked at her grandfather. He had just taken the blame for Ane's experiment. She wasn't sure if he had done that on purpose or he actually thought all this mess was the result of the temporary loss of magic.

"There is something wrong with my magic. It is not working at all, Lizzy?"

Ane watched her grandfather and mother share a look; a look Ane didn't understand. Ane's grandfather put her down on the ground. Ane nodded at George and Willow to run upstairs. They quickly did, and luckily nobody noticed them. There was far too much going on to be worried about the cat and her new friend.

"Then I will take care of this." Ane's mother recited the clean-up spell. Ane had heard this one a lot. Again, nothing happened. She tried again, but still nothing happened. She tried a third time. Nothing! Ane watched as they shared that look again.

"That's odd?" She tried again. Still nothing happened. Ane had started to wonder if the gummy bears had stolen all the magic from the house as they left. What if all the magic that was in the water was the only magic they had? What if they were drinking magic and now there was none left? It had all dried up. That was going to be bad; bad for all of them. Most of all for Ane as she hadn't even been using magic that long. That can't be fair. Although having a best friend that is a gummy bear with magic though? That really couldn't be anything bad? Having loads of gummy bear friends with magic couldn't be bad either. Could it?

"I guess we will be doing this the old-fashioned way."

Ane and her grandfather nodded. Ane walked over, and started to struggle to pick up the table in the hallway.

"Not you, Ane, it is your bedtime. Your grandfather and I will take care of this." Ane's mother took over picking up the table.

"I can help, Mum." Ane really wanted to help. There was a little bit of guilt about her grandfather taking all the blame. She felt it was the least she could do given it was all her fault.

"I know you can, but bed. I will be up to tuck you in in a little while."

Ane could tell by the tone of her voice that it wasn't a request. She gave them both a kiss and then ran up the sixty-three steps to her bedroom. She jumped onto the bed where Willow and George were already sitting.

"That was close. They didn't even notice you, George, so I think it is best you keep out of sight at the moment. I am sure by tomorrow they will discover the other gummy bears. Mum always knows everything."

George nodded in agreement. Ane had visions of her new friends creating havoc across the neighbourhood.

She knew that her door would be the first one people knocked on when something strange was happening. It always was.

"I think you should stay in the fort tonight George. I will make it for you."

Ane took out her wand and waved it at the sheets in the corner. She held her breath for a split second, worrying that magic had really been stolen from their house. It hadn't. The sheets flew across the room and made a tent in the corner. That made Ane smile with relief. Magic was still there. It was silly to think that Gummy bears could steal magic. Maybe it was just the fact that her mother and her grandfather were both just tired.

"I still have magic, Willow? See, there is nothing to worry about."

Willow wasn't worried. Ane paused, maybe she should have tried to cast the clean-up spell? She had tried it once before, but it didn't end well. In fact, it had taken her mother three clean-up spells to clean up Ane's clean-up spell. Ane told herself that it was better to keep away from it. She didn't need to see her mother any more upset.

"You can stay in there tonight, George. Tomorrow I will speak to mum and see if we can get you a real bed. Or bunk beds, bunk beds are cool."

George jumped off the bed, and ran into the fort just in time to miss her mother walk through the bedroom doors. Ane hadn't even heard the footsteps as she came up the stairs. Which was odd as she was always listening for them. Ane dived under the covers and closed her eyes as tight as she could to make out she was asleep.

"Have you brushed your teeth?"

"Yes." It wasn't technically a lie; she had brushed her teeth… yesterday. Yesterday morning, to be precise, but she had, in fact, brushed her teeth.

"Good girl. Now, sleep time, please. It has been a long day for all of us." Ane's mother walked over and gave Ane a kiss on the forehead, and then turned to walk out of the room.

"Now, put your PJs on, and brush your teeth before you go to bed… for real this time!"

Ane could hear her mother footsteps as she left the room and continued down the stairs. She jumped out of bed and did as she was told; she didn't want to upset her any more. As Ane was brushing her teeth she started to wonder again how her mother always knew everything. It must have been a spell. Something in her room maybe? Maybe there was a camera in the bedroom? A secret camera that was it. Tomorrow she was going to have to look for it. Maybe she could do a find my secret camera spell? There must have been one.

***

"Morning, dear. You were late coming to bed last night?" The queen flowed into the main breakfast hall.

"Morning, my dear." The king was at the breakfast table, but his breakfast hadn't been touched.

After the Horrible Hipolito had left, the king had tidied up The Great Hall of Books all by himself. He didn't want anyone finding out what had happened. Everything looked the same as any other day. It oddly felt the same too. He knew it wasn't though; the normality would be short-lived. A page was missing, and not just any page... a page with magic in it, on it... magic was gone! Only one wizard, The Horrible Hipolito, had magic now, and only the king knew that. This was going to mean trouble at some point. The king had no doubt about that.

The queen walked over, kissed her husband, and then sat next to him.

"Are you okay, my dear? You don't look very well? And, you are not eating your breakfast?"

"I am not hungry." The king pushed his plate away.

The queen's jaw dropped open. In their twenty years of marriage she had never heard those words from him before.

***

Fearsome Fred, Disastrous David, and Murderous Manuel were all standing around the main dining table. The Horrible Hipolito was standing in front of the stolen page which he had pinned on the wall of his cave. It was his cave; the others had squatting rights only for the last one hundred years. The Horrible Hipolito had been pointing that out to them all morning. They needed to go home.

Fearsome Fred stank. He needed to go home and take a bath. Disastrous David had drank nearly all of Horrible Hipolito's orange juice this morning, leaving less than a mouth full and putting the carton back in the fridge and Murderous Manuel, well, he was just Murderous Manuel! That was enough of a reason to want him out of his cave. The Horrible Hipolito wanted his cave back as soon as possible. They had been trespassing there for one hundred years and three days, which, for him, meant they had outstayed their welcome.

Of all the wizards, The Horrible Hipolito was the most scheming. He was also the self-proclaimed master of disguise. In relation to the others, he was actually a master of disguise, but only because he actually knew what a disguise was, and he tried to use it properly. Wizards didn't generally have a use for disguises as they could use magic to hide in plain sight. The Horrible Hipolito considered disguises to be an art form. He enjoyed the theatre and thought of himself to be a great actor. If truth be known he just wanted the attention.

The Horrible Hipolito was the unofficial leader of the wizards, well, of The Four Wizards, as neither Eric nor The Great Burtoni were considered part of their gang. It was only unofficial because if you asked the other wizards who the leader was, they would say themselves. When it came to ideas, plans, or anything else important they were supposed to do, it was The Horrible Hipolito's job to do that, but in their mind, that didn't make him their leader.

"Didn't really think this through, did you?" Fred stated, although in a very soft voice. It had been a heated discussion so far on how to break the rules of magic that were written on the page.

"Nope, didn't think it through at all." David spoke, but in an even softer voice than Fred. The Horrible Hipolito turned his stare to the table full of wizards.

"You can leave anytime you want?"

None of them replied. With The Horrible Hipolito being the only person with magic in the kingdom, the other wizards were worried about what they would do if they left. They were hardly built for work, and their biggest concern was without magic, how would they eat?

"Besides, none of you had a better idea, did you? None of you had even thought about the binding! None of you even mentioned the possibility of taking magic out of the book!"

There was mumbling from the wizards. Hipolito could hear them, he could always hear them, but he chose to ignore them this time. Wizards had a habit of mumbling when they were unhappy. When they were tired, when they were hungry. Wizards had a habit of mumbling a lot.

"So, let's go over this again, one more time." The Horrible Hipolito was now standing at the table where the other wizards were now sitting.

There was a big sigh from his audience.

"There is no magic left in the kingdom, other than with this page. So I, I mean, we, have the magic." Hipolito glanced at each of the wizards. He was expecting them to rise at his mistake, but none of them seemed to notice.

"Only when we are holding the sheet of paper!"

Hipolito gave Fred the stare... the stare that said *Say the obvious again one more time, I dare you.*

"Yes, only when we are holding the paper." The Horrible Hipolito sighed.

"And, we still have to adhere to the rules."

It was David's turn to get the stare. They were fed up with going over this again. It had got them nowhere all morning, and they were hungry again. Wizards were always hungry, food to wizards was more important than even magic.

"Yes, and we still have to adhere to the rules, David. Thanks for pointing that out... again!"

"So, yesterday we were four recently unfrozen wizards who had some magic. Today we are four recently unfrozen wizards where only one of us can have some magic, but only if they are holding the piece of paper that has magic on it... and that person still has to adhere to the same rules!"

The Horrible Hipolito didn't respond; he figured the stare was enough. He knew the situation they were in, and he also realised that he hadn't really thought this through. None of them had. Unfortunately, the other wizards blamed him for not thinking it through the most, as that was his job, and it had been his idea. Hipolito went back to the page on the wall. He took it down again and started rubbing it as if by feeling it might give him an idea on how to unlock it. The others watched.

"Hipolito?"

He knew that tone of voice. It had been the same tone of voice he had heard for the last three days. Without turning he gave a wave of his wand and a large roast chicken a bowl full of potatoes and four jugs of ale appeared on the table. He knew that that would stop the mumbling, for a while.

***

"We are going to be late…"

Owen was standing at the gate when Ane opened the door. She just laughed and caught up with him as he started down the street.

George and Willow were still hiding in the tent back in Ane's room. Ane had told them to keep away from her mother as she seemed in a mood this morning. Weirdly, so was her grandfather. Normally mornings were a very happy affair, but not this morning. There was too much silence for Ane's liking.

"Owen, it worked! The gummy bears spell, it worked!"

Owen looked at Ane in shock.

"It actually worked? I mean worked without your grandfather having to clean it all up? So, we have an endless supply of sweets?"

It was the first time Owen had ever been happy about one of Ane's experiments. It was only then that Ane remembered what they were actually trying to achieve in the first place, and how disappointed Owen was going to be.

"Ummm, well, no, it didn't actually work like that. I am still working on that one, but I am close. I made them come to life instead."

Owen stopped in his tracks. Ane didn't. It took him a minute to replay exactly what Ane had said in his head before he spoke.

"Ane, when you say come to life?"

"Yes, come to life, Owen. They can talk and everything. Oh, and they like honey, I think? Although we actually never got around to having tea. Great, eh?" Ane kept walking.

"But, Ane? They came to life?"

"Don't worry, Owen, it will be fine. George is at home with Willow now. I wanted to tell you first." Ane knew that was a little lie. She just didn't want to tell her mother, not until the house was back to normal. Besides she knew it always made Owen feel special when she involved him in her little secrets.

Owen did feel special. He also felt a little scared of Ane's little secret, but he knew there was nothing he could do now to change anything. If Ane had made talking walking gummy bears then he was just going to have to wait and see what that meant for everyone else. Owen ran up to Ane who had kept walking ahead.

"George?"

"He is my new friend, well, our new friend. George the gummy bear." Owen was still in shock.

"Just so I have this right, you made a gummy bear come to life, and called him George?"

"Yes."

Owen went silent; he was still pondering about what Ane had done.

"It's a good job that the never-ending part didn't work then. Imagine that you made a never-ending supply of gummy bear's come to life."

Ane didn't answer, although she did agree with Owen. There were a few moments over breakfast when she thought she heard a knock on the door. She was expecting neighbours to be knocking on the door wanting to speak to her, but there had been nothing. Ane was hoping that whatever happened last night was over, and George was now the only one. She ran over to the park, she climbed up the steps, and onto the slide.

"Come on, Owen."

Owen followed close behind. They each went down the slide, then they ran over to the roundabout. They spun it as fast as they could until Ane jumped off. She always jumped off first. She then headed over to the bridge. Owen had to wait for the roundabout to stop; he wasn't as brave as Ane. When the roundabout finally stopped, he stood off it safely.

"Do you want to go again?"

"No, thank you…" Owen turned, and to his surprise saw there was a gummy bear jumping on the roundabout. He stood frozen. At first, he thought it must be George. He thought George had just followed them to school, but then he looked over at the swings. There were two more

George gummy bears on the swings. He then noticed that over on the other side of the park there were about five more Georges playing with an actual football. He looked over at Ane who didn't seem to notice.

Ane *had* noticed the gummy bears when she jumped off the roundabout. At first she started getting really worried, but then she figured that they were out there now and nobody would be able to actually pinpoint this down to her. Ignoring the situation was going to be her best option.

"Ane!" Owen shouted after her, but she was already past the bridge and heading to school.

***

The king was back in The Great Hall of Books. He stood in front of the book and kept touching it. It didn't do anything; there was no glow, no floating. He picked up The Great Pen of Everything and opened the book. He wrote the word "Magic" in big bold letters on the top right-hand corner and closed the book really fast as if trapping it inside. Nothing happened. He opened the book again; the wording was still there. That wasn't going to work. He licked the pen – sometimes that made a pen work better – and tried again, and then again.

***

"Ane, there is going to be trouble! There are loads of them? Everywhere, Ane! There is even one outside the school selling sweets… sweets, Ane! Did you hear me? A gummy bear selling sweets? I was too scared to look. What if they were his toes or something? What if he chopped off his own toes, and sold them? What if they weren't his? What if they were the toes of some of the other gummy bears? What if there is a gummy bear chopping the toes and fingers off other gummy bears and selling them for money? Ane, do you even know how many of them there are?"

Ane knew that Owen's worry had reached a totally new level. It did make her smile.

"It is fine, Owen, people like gummy bears. Everyone knows that."

Ane entered the classroom. It was geography this morning which meant Mr Harrison again. Ane liked the thought of that.

"To eat, Ane. People like gummy bears to eat? They are sweets. I swear, I saw one doing a paper round on the way here? Delivering actual papers! Ane, how did he get a paper round? Even I can't get a paper round? How did a gummy bear get a paper round in less than a day? In less than half a day. More importantly what has happened to the normal paper boy?" Owen's voice had managed to get slightly higher all the way to school. At the back of Ane's mind she wondered if dogs could hear him now, and if they could, what would they say?

"Don't worry. I will speak to George when we get home and see if he can help you to get a paper round, Owen."

Owen looked at Ane. He wasn't going to be able to reason with her today, he could tell. She was already in the zone. The zone that meant she had moved on from that experiment. What was done was done. Owen was going to have to just accept it and move on.

Mr Harrison had been covering geography for the past two months while they were trying to recruit a new teacher. The teacher didn't specifically name Ane by name as the reason she had left, but she did say that in ten years of teaching she had never been asked so many times the question why? It was geography. Apparently, people don't ask why in geography. It just is.

As they sat down, Owen decided to give up trying with Ane. Some days there was no talking sense to her, and today was one of those days. He figured if she didn't notice it, then neither would he, and he tried not to think about gummy bears. Especially the sweet-selling gummy bears. Anyway, the less they spoke about them, the less chance any of this could find its way back to them.

They sat at the front of the class. Ane watched the clock as it struck nine. He was late. He was always late.

"How long do you think he will be today, Owen?"

Owen just looked at her, and shook his head.

The door to the classroom opened with a bang. They all expected it to be Mr Harrison, but a gummy bear walked in, and sat next to Ane. Ane didn't take any notice. Owen did, but he tried really hard not to. A few seconds later Mr Harrison came through the door. His head was in his book, and, as always, he had his lunch box in his hand. He sat at his desk. Ane was already on her feet to go to tell him what he was doing there today when he suddenly stood up. Today was different, he never just stood up before. Well, he stood up, but that was only when he was coming into or leaving the room. He never stood up to address the class. Generally, he would just sit at his table reading his books, sometimes eating the odd sandwich.

Ane was suddenly concerned about the gummy bear sitting next to her. She had spotted it when it walked in, she just didn't want Owen to know she had. She was sure he was going to ask her about that. Mr Harrison was clever, and he would somehow tie the two things together, her and the gummy bear. He was as powerful as her mother in that sense. Maybe he had a secret camera spell on her too.

"Where is everyone?" Ane was relieved he didn't seem to notice or acknowledge the gummy bear.

Ane turned around. There were only six people in the classroom. There should have been forty-three. Geography had forty-three. She hadn't even noticed the lack of classmates when she arrived, and neither had Owen. Owen was still fixed on the fact that there was a gummy bear selling sweets outside the school who probably only had seven toes and four fingers. All he could think about now was how he would hold the money without fingers? Also, now that there was one in the classroom with them, which nobody seemed to have noticed, Owen tried to glance over at his toes to start counting them.

Mr Harrison left the classroom, quickly followed by Ane. She followed him as he walked down the hall ways and out of the building he then headed up to the Expressway at the entrance to the school. He tapped on it. As he did that Ane realised that the only people that were in her class were the ones that lived close to the school. That's why she didn't notice on the way to school; she saw the same people she always saw.

The Express Way wasn't working. Mr Harrison must have noticed that straightaway. He tapped it again. He reached into his pocket and then suddenly stopped. He pulled out his hand, but there was nothing in it. He turned and headed back to the classroom. Ane was right behind him. She was going to say something, but he didn't look happy. He walked into the classroom and sat back at his desk. Ane was expecting him to pick up a book and start reading, but he didn't. Ane stood in the doorway looking at the class. She whispered over to Owen, and he repeated her words straight back to her

"The Express Way isn't working?" Owen almost shouted the words as Ane shrugged her shoulders.

They all waited for a response from Mr Harrison, but he just sat there staring blankly at the classroom. Ane eventually sat back down next to Owen. The gummy bear got up and left, but still nobody said a word. Everyone was still fixated on their teacher.

"Class dismissed." Mr Harrison got up, picked up his lunch box, his book, and left the classroom.

Everyone else remained seated, even Ane, for a short while. Class had never been dismissed before. Did that mean just this class or the whole school? Ane ran after Mr Harrison.

"Sir, sir, what does that mean? What does 'class dismissed' mean?"

"It means go home, Ane. School is closed."

That stopped Ane in her tracks. School is closed. These were words Ane only dreamed of. Ane ran back to the classroom to tell everyone. They were all in a huddle in the middle of the classroom, well, as much as a few people can make a huddle.

"School is closed."

Ane expected a huge cheer. There wasn't one.

"James says that magic has gone. His mum told him that magic has disappeared from the kingdom?" Owen was keen to get Ane up to speed on what they were talking about as soon as she was back in the room

James the Giant just nodded.

"That is why the portal doesn't work. There is no magic left."

"That's just silly, of course there is magic. Look!" Ane flicked her hand, and her chair moved.

There was a gasp from the whole class, well, from the other four people in the room and Owen.

"James says that his mother and grandmother lost their magic last night? They can't do anything today?"

James the Giant nodded again. It was all he could do. He could never speak in front of Ane; she scared him. He was a six-foot-four giant, but even though Ane was little, she had always scared him. Especially when she had her wand in her hand.

James the Giant's mother and grandmother were witches. His dad had been a giant, a six-foot-four giant, but a giant nonetheless.

Ane thought back to last night. Her mother couldn't do magic either. She had spent the whole night cleaning up Ane's mess. Her grandfather, his magic disappeared mid spell. That was something that had never happened before. There was definitely something going on.

"Owen, we have to go." Ane grabbed Owen by the hand, and ran out of the classroom. They ran all the way to the history block.

"Ane, what are we doing here?"

Ane was looking at the wall through the history of The Great Wizards.

"My mother and grandfather didn't have magic last night either. I thought it was because they were tired, but James might be on to something."

"Oh! But... you still have magic, Ane? How is that? Why would you be the only person with magic, Ane?" Owen paused. Of course she would be the only person with magic. If magic were to disappear from the world, Ane would be at the centre of it somewhere.

"What else did you do last night, Ane?" Owen's mind had been on overdrive today. Ane was the only person left with magic, so the first thing that naturally came to his mind was that she had done something, maybe a spell. A spell collecting up all the magic in the kingdom? That was something Ane would be working on.

"Nothing. I haven't done anything." Ane carried on looking at the walls.

Owen wasn't convinced, but he did trust her. To this day, he never thought that she had lied to him. That is not what best friends do.

"Oh, okay. What are we doing here then, Ane?"

Ane was silent. She had heard the tone in his voice when he asked what else she had done. She was starting to wonder the same thing. Maybe all this was something to do with her, with her spell. Maybe it had something to do with the gummy bears. Ane was back to thinking if they could have taken magic from the world?

She needed answers, and this was the place she always came for answers. Ane stayed focused on the walls. They were covered with the history of the kingdom. Maybe there was something about creating life? Maybe that was one of the rules she had forgotten? By doing what she did, she may have broken a fundamental rule. That was surely strong magic she used yesterday. Maybe her spell was the cause of removing magic from the kingdom.

Ane re-read everything she could. She couldn't see anything on creating life.

As she was reading, something else started to stand out at her. It had been the one-hundred-year anniversary of The Great Wizards' disappearance only a few days ago. That couldn't be a coincidence. It might not be her, after all; it might have something to do with that… with them! Ane had even started a rumour a few weeks ago that they may return after one hundred years. It had totally slipped from her mind since then. Now she was starting to think that it might actually be true. Something was happening to magic one hundred years after real magic had disappeared from their lives forever. Ane was suddenly aware that Owen was still standing next to her, waiting for an answer to his question.

"It helps me think to be here, Owen. We need to work out what is going on."

***

Mr Harrison was back in his own office in the school. The room was full of books; books of all genres. They were stacked in every corner of the room. He had read most of them. Not start to finish, but he always seemed to know where he left off last time he dropped the book.

Ane didn't know that he had returned to the history block as well or she would have run after him to ask him questions. If anyone knew about this stuff it would be Mr Harrison.

Mr Harrison packed some of his books into a suitcase as carefully as he could, and picked up his lunch box. After a short moment of hesitation he turned and picked up his spare lunch box, the one he used in case of emergencies. Once he had everything he needed, he left the history block through a side door, to avoid attracting unwanted attention.

***

Ane's grandfather walked into the kitchen where her mother was sitting at the kitchen table looking concerned. He sat down next to her and grabbed her hand, to comfort her.

"It is true, Lizzy. Magic has gone. I can't get anything to work and neither can any of our neighbours."

They were silent for a while.

"You don't think that?"

"I don't know Lizzy, but we have to consider it."

They sat in silence a little longer. Then without speaking, they both got up and left the kitchen together.

Chapter 7

The Four Wizards were all now sat at the table. The roast chicken was gone, and so was the pasta, the beef, roast potatoes, chocolate cake, and the roasted pears. There were still some Brussels sprouts on the table, but nobody, not even Fred wanted them. The Horrible Hipolito was glad of that. There didn't need to be any more foreign smells in his cave. He didn't want to, but The Horrible Hipolito kicked off the conversation again.

"There must be a way, a way to change the rules that The Great Burtoni has laid down. He is really starting to make me quite angry. Who calls themselves The Great anyway? It is hardly scary. What made him so great?"

All the wizards looked blankly at each other.

"Maybe the fact that he can do magic we can't undo?"

Everyone turned their attention to Fred. There was quite a bit of mumbling under their breaths at this point.

"Well, there isn't, is there? We have tried everything."

They had tried everything. Well, everything four wizards with very little imagination could think of. They had tried to change it with the little magic they had, but nothing. They tried writing on it, but still nothing. Hipolito did think about getting The Great Pen of Everything from the palace. Although he was sure that wasn't going to work either. He knew Burtoni; he would have never left real magic in the hands of a king. It was one thing to let him think he was in control, but he would have never allowed a king to change the rules of magic, it was too important to him. No matter how much he disliked what the other wizards had been doing to the kingdom.

"Burtoni would have had a way, I know him. He would not leave anything to chance, he would know how to change the rules."

What the The Horrible Hipolito had said was true, he did know him. They actually all knew each other very well. The wizards were never really at war with each other. They were always just trying to show how good they were. It was always more of a game to them. They would even get together in secret once a month to discuss what was going on in the kingdom, and talk about their latest achievements. It was why there were so many wars that lasted only a couple of days, some were a matter of hours. After a few glasses of ale they would tell each other what they were planning, then go home and work on counteract spells against each other.

In the early days before The Great Burtoni started writing the book, he would come along to the meetings. The wars never interested him, but as he was classed as one of the great wizards, he felt that meant he needed to attend just to keep up appearances. He never joined in any of the long debates about the kingdom or with any of the baking challenges. This upset Manuel. Manuel had started the baking to try to make it more of a social event to ensure they all remained friends. That, and because eating was the most important thing in the kingdom to a wizard even before magic. Magic was a very close second. Every month they would bring something nice to eat. All of them except for The Great Burtoni. He never cooked. After years of meetings the most they ever got from him was a sandwich. Manuel was convinced that had only been because the bread was out of date and he had wanted to use it up. Manuel hadn't eaten the sandwich out of principle. Nobody noticed.

"Let's go and ask him then?"

It was Manuel's turn to get everyone's attention and set off their mumbling again.

"I am just saying! Where is he anyway?"

"Maybe he is dead?"

Nobody in the room believed him to be dead. Not even Fred. He knew they were the wrong words as soon as they came out of his mouth.

"He is too stubborn for that. He will be around here somewhere."

"The people are saying that he disappeared shortly after us so maybe he is frozen too?"

The Horrible Hipolito was shaking his head.

"David, how do you know what the people are saying? You haven't left the cave in a hundred years? What people? Who said this?"

Disastrous David looked down at the floor whilst mumbling that Fred had told him. The Horrible Hipolito was the only person that heard him.

"Think about it. Why would he be frozen? We were frozen because somewhere in *The Great Big Book of Everything and Cheese and Onion Sandwiches*, stupid name... and by the way, seeing that title is how I knew The Great Burtoni will have something that is able to modify *The Great Big Book of...* okay, I am sick of it, let's just call it the book from now on, that title is driving me mad. Anyway, back to the matter at hand, inside the book, somewhere, there must be a spell saying that if we were going to change or harm life we would be frozen for a hundred years. He would not then go and make that mistake, would he?"

The wizards all shook their heads. That did make sense.

"What about Eric? Eric wouldn't have hurt anyone, would he?"

They all turned to look at Manuel. He didn't speak very often. Generally, because the others would disregard whatever he said, and for a good reason.

"Eric, what are you going on about?"

"Eric wouldn't be frozen, would he? He has never hurt anyone?"

"What does that have to do with anything? We are talking about the rules and The Great Burtoni? Idiot! Eric is a rabbit. He is probably hopping around in the woods somewhere, making giant carrots."

Manuel went back to silence.

"No. Burtoni will have had a way to change the pages of the book. I am sure it will be in his house. That's where he wrote it, so it must be there. I think the best thing we can do is take a trip to his house."

The wizards nodded. It was all that they could think of. It was all Hipolito could think of and that was good enough for them.

"Wait a minute, do you know how far that is?"

They all looked at Manuel, for once he had a valid point.

***

"The Great Burtoni was born just the other side of the Horningdale wood. How didn't I know that, Owen? I would have gone to his house if I had known that. It says here, to Harrold and Martha Burtoni. I always thought..." Ane stopped in mid flow.

"I know what it is! I hope that James has not gone home yet. Come with me, Owen."

Ane ran out of the history block with Owen following closely behind.

"James! James!" Two minutes later Ane was screaming across the school field at him.

He could hear her, he just wasn't sure that he wanted to stop so he carried on walking. He knew that Ane coming after you screaming your name generally meant trouble. Eventually she caught up with him. She was really fast for a little girl despite how big he had made his stride.

"James, come with me…" Ane grabbed him by the hand and started to lead him back to the school.

It was times like this when James wished that he wasn't so scared of her. Unfortunately, he was, so he just followed her. Minutes later they were back in the classroom. Ane ran to the corner of the room and pulled out the creative box taking out a tape measure. She then placed James next to the table and climbed up and stood on the table. They were now close to the same size .

"Owen, grab this end." Ane pulled the bottom of the tape measure out and gestured towards Owen. He did as he was told. Everyone did as they were told when Ane was in this mode.

"Now Owen, hold it at James's feet." Owen looked at James. They both had the look of boys who were worried about the outcome of this experiment. How bad could it be though? It was only a tape measure? But it was Ane with a tape measure. Owen did as he was told. Ane then held the tape at the top of James's head.

"I knew it! I knew I was right!" Ane let go of the tape which dropped onto Owen's hand.

"Sorry!" Ane jumped off the table.

"What was right? Ane, what were you right about?" Owen reeled the tape measure back in.

"Magic! It is all about the magic. James, your mother was right."

Ane was pacing around in a circle. Owen was now getting worried. He had seen Ane do this before. There was a plan forming, a serious plan. This pacing generally meant that something was about to happen, something that could have disastrous implications for some people. At this moment, he just hoped they weren't for him, Ane, or James, who was looking more worried by the minute.

"What are you talking about, Ane?"

Ane looked at Owen and then at James. James just nodded in return. He didn't know what else to do.

"Don't you see, Owen? Magic has gone from the kingdom. My mother and grandfather couldn't do magic last night either. It all makes sense."

"But you can? I saw you?" Owen wasn't sure that made any sense.

"Yes, but I was locked in my grandfather's trunk. You know, the *no magic in, no magic out trunk*? I was protected. Someone or something has taken magic away from the kingdom!"

Owen wasn't quite following what Ane was saying, but he was trying.

"Why were you locked in your grandfather's trunk, Ane?"

"It doesn't matter; it was just to do with the hundreds of gummy bears running all over the house. Don't you see? It must have something to do with *The Great Big Book of Everything and Cheese and Onion Sandwiches*. What if magic has been taken out? Or the book has been stolen or destroyed? What if the wizards have returned? What if there are new wizards? What if I am the Last Witch in the kingdom?" Ane couldn't keep still. Her mind was running as fast as her feet now.

"Hundreds of gummy bears? Ane, there are hundreds of gummy bears out there? Alive ones? And they were all in your house?"

"Yes, that's it... the book! Magic must have been taken out of the book somehow? The king must have opened it, but why would he take magic out? Surely he knows the kingdom is a better place with magic in it?" Ane was pacing even quicker now. Her mind was in overdrive. Then, suddenly, she stopped and stood still. She didn't move for what seemed like ages to the others. It seemed like ages as they were all holding their breath whilst she stood still.

Owen knew that meant that she had a plan. He wished at that point she was still walking.

"We need some supplies from home, and then we will go to The Great Burtoni's house." James and Owen both took a breath.

"I thought you said the king had done something? Doesn't that mean that something has happened at the palace?" Owen was catching up fast.

"I did, but first we need to go there to see if there are any clues about where he went. We may need him to fix this. Then we can go to the palace. We need to at least try to put magic back in the book." In truth, Ane knew that The Great Burtoni's house was en route to the palace, and now that she knew where it was, she just wanted to go visit it.

"But, Ane, do you know how far that is? It is a long way to the palace."

Ane wasn't in the mood for buts, not today. Today she had a plan. The most exciting, amazing plan ever.

"No buts, Owen. Someone has to take care of this and it is going to be me... well, us, Willow, and George. George will love the adventure; between us we can do this. It will be fine Owen." Ane was focused, confident and positive. Owen knew that meant trouble, he didn't know when but he knew it would find them

James took a step back from the table. He hadn't heard his name, but he was still worried that she might include him in this adventure. She didn't look over at him. That was a good sign and came as a huge relief, he had played his part in Ane's new adventure.

"But, Ane..."

"Owen, it will be fine. It is always fine. We will be fine. Come on." Ane was already heading towards the door.

"Okay, okay Ane, but at least tell us what the tape and James were for?"

"Oh, that! He is six foot five and a half. The giants have started growing again. That is how I knew there is something wrong with *The Great Big Book of Everything and Cheese and Onion Sandwiches*."

Ane was already out the door when Owen handed the tape measure to James who was grinning from ear to ear. Not only was he happy at the fact that he was now six foot five and a half, but he was also smiling because that was the least painful session with Ane ever.

***

The four wizards left the cave. The Horrible Hipolito thought about making sure they all took a shower before they left, but it was his bathroom and he didn't want Fred cleaning himself in it. No matter how much he needed it.

When The Great Burtoni had cast his spell across the kingdom, the four wizards had met to come up with a plan. They knew their plan of destroying the book was going to need all their magic combined, but even together, the spell they had cast had not been strong enough. They turned their attention to The Great Burtoni himself that had been a mistake a mistake they had been realising for the last one hundred years that they had been frozen in The Horrible Hipolito's cave. The Great Burtoni had done a good job of protecting the book, and the people, from the wizards' magic. Burtoni knew it was mainly the kings who were responsible for most of the evil doings across the lands, but he also knew it was easier to restrict the wizards' magic than it was to stop the imagination of kings and queens.

Sewn into the border of the page that The Horrible Hipolito had in his top pocket, if they had taken the time to look closely enough, was, in fact, the spell. It was written so small that you could hardly see the words. It looked more like a decorative pattern. Any wizard or witch using magic to change the fate of any loyal subject of the kingdom would be frozen for a hundred years. He thought that would be long enough to teach them a lesson. The Four Wizards had been frozen together in the cave the moment they tried to do the spell.

Eric, on the other hand, had been frozen in the woods. That's why nobody had seen him. He had been concentrating on creating a giant carrot, not noticing the man heading through the forest on horseback. Neither the horse nor the man saw the twenty-foot carrot springing up from the ground in front of them. The man fell and broke his left ankle and his right leg. Eric, being Eric, decided to help him, as he felt partly responsible for him running straight into his lunch. The Great Burtoni, in hindsight, could have made the spell better. Eric had interfered with the fate of a loyal subject by healing his wounds, so he had been frozen as well. He wasn't as upset about it as The Horrible Hipolito though, probably because he didn't have Fred to look at and smell for a hundred years. That wasn't the worse thing. The Horrible Hipolito had dropped his pen right before casting the spell. Seeing and smelling Fred from that angle for one hundred years still gave him nightmares.

Eric had had one paw on his carrot when he was frozen, which led to the carrot being frozen with him. There were worse things he could spend a hundred years looking at than his lunch. He had spent the last one hundred years imagining how good it was going to taste.

"I miss magic..."

"Shut up, Fred!" The wizards spoke in unison.

"You would have thought that during all the years that we were fighting each other and coming up with new magical experiments to outdo each other, we would have at least come up with some kind of transportation device. Something other than horseback and walking; I hate walking." Manuel was making sure that the sound of his stomping on the ground was heard by all as he said that.

"You would have thought The Great Burtoni would have remembered horses. Horses! They are hardly ants. How did he remember ants, and he didn't remember horses?"

All the wizards shook their heads.

"Where did the horses go? I mean I know he forgot them but did they just disappear? Wouldn't they just reappear now if that was the case? Or do they need to breed again. How are they going to breed if there are no horses to start with? What are people going to do if they see a horse now? They would be scared? Imagine a horse coming towards you for the first time" Everyone stopped and looked at Manuel. That was a lot of information to take in is such a short time. They all decided it was easier to tut and shake their heads. It was the response he was used too.

"I remember when we didn't need horses. We just transported ourselves. Quick wave of the old..." David whipped his hand above his head.

"With Magic" Manuel opened his mouth again. "Yes, with magic." Manuel seemed pleased he wasn't shouted down and this time acknowledged for his input.

"I miss magic." He tried his luck one more time.

"Shut up, Manuel!"

They all continued to walk in silence.

***

"But, Ane, someone else will sort it out? Why does it always have to be you?" Owen had tried to dissuade Ane from the trip. If she went, he knew he was going to have to go too. They were best friends and that is what best friends do. Follow you no matter what trouble you get in.

"Who, Owen? I am the only person with magic in the village. I am probably the only person with magic in the whole kingdom. Nobody else can sort it out. This time it has to be me." There was a beaming smile across Ane's face as she said that.

Owen didn't have an answer for her this time. He knew that she could very well be right as frightening as that sounded to him.

"I am sure the king has just made a mistake and probably tore the page out or spilled some mustard on it."

They both laughed.

Every picture in the kingdom of the king had him very close to some kind of food, and there was always mustard on his robe or the collar of his shirt.

"There is probably some glue or something in Burtoni's house that we can use to stick it back in." Ane was stretching. She just wanted to go to his house. Even if magic hadn't disappeared, she would have been going to his house now she knew where it was. Ane finished packing all her magic related things in her bag. The beakers, the tubes, and even the old shoe... she even emptied her secret stash of treats even though she still had today's lunch packed as school had been closed. Ane picked up her training wand. She spent a few minutes looking at it, and then placed it back onto the side.

"Wait here." Ane ran down the stairs and into the basement. She went straight to the trunk, and pulled out her grandfather's wand. She had never been allowed to use it. She wasn't even sure it would work for her, but what she did know was that it wouldn't work for anyone else. She also knew she was probably going to need real magic in order to fix this.

Ane, Willow, George, and her grandfather's wand were the only things that had been protected last night from whatever had happened. Ane ran back to her bedroom.

"Okay, I have everything."

Owen watched as she placed the wand in the bag. He didn't say anything; he knew there was no point. He was going to have to go with Ane to protect her, from herself. The wand was just something else for Owen to worry about. Along with the toe-eating, finger-munching gummy bears that were he was 100% sure were not going to be everywhere.

"Come on, George, and you, Willow."

George and Willow came out of the fort. They looked as enthusiastic as Owen to be going on the adventure. Truth be told, Willow looked as enthusiastic as Owen, George just smiled. He was always smiling. There was nothing for a gummy bear to worry about in life. Well, unless you were a gummy bear in Owen's mind right now... bumping into the gummy bear selling sweets outside the school. Then he should be scared. Very scared.

"Hello, Owen." George came up and shook Owens hand as if they had been best friends for ever.

"Hello, George."

Owen watched as George the gummy bear followed Ane out of the room, followed slowly by Willow. Owen sighed in resignation and hurried up after them. His plan to try to get someone else to deal with this had failed. They were all going on the adventure, Willow, Ane, Himself and the walking talking gummy bear George.

***

"Are we nearly there yet?"

It had been the third time that question had been asked in the last ten minutes. The Horrible Hipolito was leading them as always, which also ensured that he stayed upwind from the rest of them. From time to time his mind marvelled at the freshness of the clean air in his nostrils.

"We have been walking for twenty minutes!"

The Horrible Hipolito stopped in his tracks. Wizards weren't known for their fitness, or their patience, for that matter.

"Tomorrow! We will be there tomorrow; I told you that. We even discussed how long tomorrow was; Manuel counted the hours. How he got to thirty-seven hours in a day, I will never know, but that was only twenty minutes ago. It took us two hours plus another lunch to finally leave our cave, my cave! To leave my cave." Hipolito took a deep breath.

"There is somewhere for us to stop on the way. Now shut up the lot of you." Hipolito stomped off in front of them.

"If I had magic…"

"But you don't, Fred! You don't have magic." Hipolito shouted behind him.

Fred, Manuel, and David went quiet. Well, they kept quiet until they thought he had gone far enough ahead. A few minutes later, when they were sure that Hipolito couldn't hear them they started speaking again.

"How did the cranky old git hear that?"

"I hear everything!" Hipolito shouted at the top of his voice.

The wizards glared grumpily forward, and went quiet again.

***

"She has gone." Ane's mother came down the stairs as her grandfather came up from the basement. "She has taken all her equipment, and even her secret stash of food."

"She has taken my wand as well."

"How is this happening? I thought we were safe. I thought we had thought of everything." Ane's mother sounded like she was about to cry.

They shared a hug standing in the hall way.

"You don't know anything is happening. She may have just gone off to the Dip or on one of her quick adventures as school has been closed. Owen wouldn't let her get into too much trouble." He tried to comfort her, but deep down inside he had the same feeling...It had started!

"Let's go and check, shall we?"

Ane's mother nodded. They both entered the basement, and walked down the stairs. They walked over to the trunk. Ane's grandfather changed the eight digit dial to number twenty-seven, and opened the case. Without a word they both stepped inside the case, and walked down the long set of stairs that we inside.

***

"Ane, it's a long walk. That is why we have the Express Way. I am just saying."

"We don't have the Express Way anymore, Owen, we have to walk. It will be fine."

The Express Way had been a gift from The Great Burtoni a day before he made *The Great Big Book of Everything and Cheese and Onion sandwiches* live across the Kingdom. He had been working on the spell in secret so that the other wizards didn't find out. It would have been something that all Wizards and kings would have given anything for. The magic to take you anywhere in the Kingdom. He had known for a long time it was possible because he had seen it in use once before, but he was very young and it was a powerful spell completed by a very powerful Wizard.

Owen wasn't convinced. She always told him it would be fine. It was like an instant reaction to everything and anything Owen ever said to her.

George and Willow were walking about five feet behind them. Owen was still amazed at the thought of a gummy bear being with them. He kept looking around to check he was still there and he was still real. He had a real urge to poke him just to check but he figured that might be rude. As gummy bears go though, he was a nice one. He was the nicest talking, walking gummy bear that Owen had ever spent any time with. He was very polite, and he didn't seem to be worried about anything; although that part was a little worrying for Owen. Other than that, he was just a nice gummy bear. Owen had counted his toes and fingers though – three times. Thankfully, they were all there. Owen had thought to himself how tempting it would be to eat your own toes if you were a gummy bear. He didn't like the fact that he had thought about it, but he thought about it all the same.

***

The king was in the kitchen watching Cook prepare the food. He had been sitting at the table for twenty minutes, but hadn't said a word. What was more worrying to Cook was that he hadn't asked for any food either, even after he had skipped breakfast for the first time in his life.

Nothing else had happened though. Magic had gone and nobody seemed to notice. Well nobody he had met had seemed to notice. Was anything really going to happen? The king couldn't stop thinking about that. Maybe it was all going to work out, and maybe, just maybe, the kingdom no longer needed *The Great Big Book of Everything and Cheese and Onion Sandwiches*. Maybe it had played its part in history, and now it was time to move on. The king kept going over that point in his head over and over again. It was time to move on.

"Cook."

Cook turned around with a questioning expression. At last, it was time to find out what the king wanted to eat. He wouldn't have been in the kitchen if he didn't want some kind of food.

"Have you ever heard of pickle?"

The word took the cook by surprise.

"No, sire."

The king looked disappointed. He was sure if anyone knew what pickle was, it would have been Cook. She must have been around one hundred years ago, when The Horrible Hipolito had told him it used to be around? A few minutes later he spoke again.

"What about a knickerbocker glory?"

"No, sire. What is it?" Cook was now standing in front of him.

"It is something to do with iced cream, which I can only presume is cream with ice in it or frozen cream like ice? And chocolate, and peanuts, and sauce... lots of sauce. Lots of different flavours like strawberry, raspberry, and bubble gum. Umm, I don't know what bubble gum is, but doesn't it sound delicious? Bubble, bubbles sounds funny, right?"

Cook just stared at him, wondering where these new words had come from. If there was one thing Cook knew about the king, it was that he wasn't a new word kind of king, especially when it came to food, and he was always talking about food.

"It does sound... interesting? Do you want me to try to make it?"

The king sat and thought for a moment. Nothing has gone wrong, nothing has changed since the page was taken out. It will be fine. It was time to move on.

"Yes, I think so."

Cook turned to get on with making her first knickerbocker glory, she also started to ponder what bubble gum was, the king was right it did sound funny. Cook just didn't know how she could make it?

***

"Ane, are you sure this is the right way?"

Ane just nodded at Owen. She wasn't sure. It was further than they had ever walked in the woods before. In fact, they had never actually walked into the woods before, not even on Eric's day. Ane's and Owen's mothers would hide the carrots on the outside of the forest as they were worried Owen would be too scared to go hunting for them. There was a path; surely that meant that it led through the woods to somewhere? It was a logical expectation, that is what Ane had comforted Owen with.

"It's a little dark, Ane."

It was still afternoon, but it was getting late. The main reason it was a little dark was because they were heading into the thick of the woods. The branches were starting to block out the sun. Ane took out her grandfather's wand and lit the sky above them. It happened straightaway. It was the first time Owen had ever seen a magic spell work for Ane that quickly. He looked at Ane in amazement, he instantly saw that she was as surprised as he was, although she was trying to hide it. That started to worry him, but not Ane, she just carried on walking as if it was natural.

***

Ane's mother and grandfather entered the cave.

"They are gone." Ane's mother gave a huge sigh. She had feared this was going to happen.

"They have been unfrozen."

"Yes, it would seem so" Ane's grandfather put a comforting arm on her shoulder.

"Then it is happening. I knew they weren't going to stay like that forever. I told you that."

Ane's grandfather was nodding his head. Deep down, he knew it too. He had checked up on them often over the last one hundred years. Careful never to be seen, he just checked that all four of them were still there. Nobody knew of the spell or how long they would be frozen other than The Great Burtoni.

They both knew of the prophecy though. All the wizards and witches knew of the prophecy. They knew what was coming next.

"We have to find Ane."

They both nodded their heads and entered the door that had appeared in the corner of the cave less than a few minutes ago. As they started to climb the stairs the doorway vanished behind them.

***

"Cook, mmm! This is the best thing I have ever tasted. It is amazing."

Cook looked pleased with herself and confused at the same time. She hadn't managed to make the bubble gum. She had tried, but figured that what she had made wasn't to be eaten. It was still stuck to the inside of one of her saucepans, and she was sure it was never coming back out.

"What I don't understand sire is why I didn't make it before? I am always trying to think of new recipes. Iced cream, why had I never been able to think about that?"

The king was too engrossed in the knickerbocker glory to hear her question. Cook went back to the side, and started thinking of other things she could try. Something came to her straight away. Without a word she went over to the pantry, pulled out the butter, a big bag of peanuts, and sat them on the side next to her.

"Butter and peanuts."

"Peanut butter!"

Cook could just about make out what the king had said with his mouth full of creamed ice.

Cook took out her ladle, and got to work.

***

"Ane!"

Ane was walking ahead of the three of them now. Owen thought it was better to keep George and Willow company for a while. There was safety in numbers, plus they were probably scared and needed his protection. That was Owens excuse. Seeing Ane create magic first time had started to worry him. Something had changed in her too. She had more purpose than ever. Owen stopped in his tracks.

"Ane!" Owen shouted again. "Ane!"

Ane turned around at the third time of calling, yelling from Owen.

"It will be fine, Owen."

Owen was standing still and pointing into the woods. Ane turned to see an opening. The sun had burst through the opening and was glistening against something that looked like a massive rock of gold. It sparkled as the sun shone on it.

"It looks like a great big golden piece of…"

"Carrot."

They all turned to George. George just smiled, happy with the answer that he had given. He didn't really know what a carrot looked like. The word had just appeared in his head. He was right. Just sitting there, in the middle of the woods, was a twenty-foot carrot.

Chapter 8

"Who knew peanuts and butter would taste so good together?" Cook stood looking at the buttered peanuts. She took another spoonful. It stuck her tongue to the roof of her mouth. It was amazing. She looked over at the sausages cooking in the pan. Hot sausages and peanut butter, who would have thought it?

The king was at the table. There was creamed ice on his chin and an empty bowl in front of him. He was waiting patiently for what was to come next.

"Are we sure about this, Cook?"

Cook took the sausages from the pan and sliced them in half. She then placed them into the bread spread with peanut butter.

"I am not sure, sire. I mean, a sausage and peanut butter sandwich? Doesn't sound natural, but here it is, here it is in front of me! How did that happen? Or more importantly, why didn't it happen before today?"

She looked over at the king as he sat at the table. The king looked happier than she had ever seen him. She was sure it was because of all the new food he was tasting. This was turning out to be a great day the king thought as she handed him the sandwich. Suddenly though, Cook's face changed. The king noticed it straight away. There wasn't just confusion on her face now... now there was something else.

"Yes, dear, how has that happened? Today of all days?"

The king knew that voice, and he knew the tone of that voice meant that she wasn't happy about finding him there. It wasn't a loud voice, in fact, it was soft and gentle. That was the voice she used when she was really serious.

"There seems to be a few hundred people upstairs, my dear, who would like to have a word with you; apparently, something has happened in the Kingdom?"

The king looked at the sandwich in front of him. He didn't know whether to turn around to his wife or pick it up to give it a big bite. There was a good chance she wasn't going to allow him to eat it if he turned around, and he would have to leave the kitchen. Surprising himself though, he turned to face the queen.

***

"What is it?"

Ane, Owen, George, and Willow were stood looking at the great orange glow in the distance. George and Willow weren't actually looking at the glow, more looking at the others looking at the great orange glow in the distance. They had a mild interest, but not a real one.

"I don't know? I know what it looks like?"

Owen knew Ane enough to know what the next action was. She started walking straight towards it.

"Ane…" Before the rest of the sentence *Don't you think we should…* came out of his mouth, he already knew the words that were coming out of Ane's.

"It will be fine, Owen."

Owen caught up with her as she reached the glistening statue.

"I think it is frozen? Look, Owen, touch it."

"Ane…"

It was too late, Ane's hand was already on the ice. "See, frozen! Frozen and wet, maybe it is melting in the sun?"

Owen didn't touch it. George and Willow did though. George even licked it. It was cold, but it tasted quite nice. George gave it a couple more licks just to check, which then incentivised Willow who thought it would be okay to lick it too.

"It's a frozen carrot in the middle of the woods? Why would a frozen…" Ane had disappeared around the other side of the carrot when she suddenly stopped talking.

"Ane?"

There was silence. Owen didn't like it when Ane stopped mid-sentence. He ran around to the other side of the giant carrot. He found Ane stood completely still as if she was now frozen, looking at what was in front of her. It was a frozen rabbit. Not just a frozen rabbit, but a frozen rabbit wearing a wizard's hat.

***

"Fine, we can stop here for the evening, but it will take us longer tomorrow. I am just putting it out there one more time. It's not even teatime yet." The Horrible Hipolito looked at the three overly tired wizards. He had had enough of their bickering for one day.

They had reached the Horse and Cart Inn. They hadn't planned to stay there for the night. There was another inn about another two-hours' walk away, but The Horrible Hipolito was sure they weren't going to make it that far, not in one piece anyway. The other wizards looked happy with this decision. It was the first time they had looked happy since leaving the cave. They all walked into the tavern together. The place was full of local people. There was a band playing, and a log fire burning. Smiles came across all the wizards' faces as they walked in, the thought of food and ale had them all happy.

. The whole tavern fell silent, turned, and looked at the four strangers. In return, the wizards all looked at each other. In hindsight, The Horrible Hipolito thought shortly afterwards, they should have probably removed the pointy hats before walking in. It was such a giveaway who they were.

***

"Is that who I think it is?" Owen was now holding Ane's hand.

"I think so. I think it is!" Owen could hear the excitement in Ane's voice as she spoke.

"Really?"

Owen and Ane stood for a moment looking at each other in amazement.

"Yes, I think so Owen." Ane held out her other hand to touch the frozen rabbit.

"Ane!" Owen called out loudly. He wasn't sure touching him was a good idea.

She instinctively pulled her hand back quickly from the ice which shocked Owen, which even shocked herself. She was now looking directly at him. That had never happened before; she had never been nervous before. Then, she let go of his hand and stood forward.

"It will be fine." She turned and tapped at the ice around the frozen rabbit. As she did, she heard the first crack, and then another, and another it was getting louder...

Ane took three steps back. The rest of her team took five. Owen took six just to be safe. The cracking continued until there was a loud crash. All the ice fell from the carrot and the rabbit at the same time. Ane took another step back. Owen, George, and Willow were now ten steps behind her, hiding behind a tree. Ane waited looking excitedly in front of her.

Slowly the rabbit started to move, then it hopped out from the ice circle around it and shook itself.

"That was cold."

Ane stood in silence. The rabbit hopped over towards her.

"Hi, I am Eric."

For the second time in her life Ane felt as if she was lost for words. Eric the wizard was standing right in front of her.

***

"I can just explain, dear, you see…"

"It is not me you are going to have to explain to, my dear."

The queen was walking up the stairs in front of the king. He was trying hard to keep up with her, but it wasn't easy. She was a lot fitter than him, plus she wasn't trying to eat a peanut butter and sausage sandwich as she climbed the stairs. He had grabbed it as he had been ordered, very politely, to follow her up the stairs. He figured he could finish the sandwich by the time they reached the top of the stairs and she wouldn't even notice.

"I was tricked."

The queen stopped and looked at him. He quickly hid the sandwich behind his back. She didn't say anything, but she didn't have to, the look was enough. She turned and started to walk on. The king walked behind her, a little slower this time. They reached the top of the stairs and headed to the main hall. The guards pushed the doors open as soon as they saw them approach, and as they did, the king could hear the noise. Hundreds of voices, all at once. He was starting to get a dreaded feeling that something did actually happen when he opened the book last night. Everything wasn't going to be okay after all.

***

Ane's mother and grandfather were back in front of the trunk in their basement. Without saying anything Ane's grandfather spun the dials once more to 00000042. There was a clunking and clattering sound and then the noise stopped. He lifted the lid and they stepped back in and walked down the stairs once more.

***

The four wizards sat at the table in the corner, each with a flagon of ale. The tavern was a lot less noisy than when they had first walked in. In fact, there was barely a sound. Most of the people in the tavern were talking in whispers to each other.

"Nice place, good beer."

They all turned to look at Fred. He wasn't paying attention to what was going on around him. Probably because nobody was actually around them; they were all on the other side of the tavern. Fred was so used to people keeping their distance from him that he had not noticed.

"They know, don't they?" Even Manuel had worked it out.

"Yes, they know, but it doesn't matter. They won't do anything. We are four of The Six. They will be more scared of us than we are of them."

"I wouldn't be so sure, I am pretty scared." David sat a little further back in the corner than all of them.

Some of the people in the bar were starting to point. The Horrible Hipolito could pick up their whispers; they were all talking about them and linking it to the fact that magic had disappeared. The waitress came over and brought their food. She put it down softly, and slowly reversed away from the table almost bowing as she did.

"Thank you." Fred was smiling at the food as she had placed it down.

The waitress just nodded. The wizards tucked in to the food. It may have been a little uncomfortable in the tavern , but nothing kept a wizard from his dinner.

***

"Hi."

Ane was still staring at a real-life One of The Six. This was something she had always dreamed about, plus, Eric was her favourite too. Well, next to The Great Burtoni... Actually, if truth be told, she also had a soft spot for Manuel. If someone had asked her why she would have struggled to say answer, but deep down she knew it was because he messed up most of the spells that he cast, especially ones that included disappearing spells. They had become legendary. He was so bad at casting them that people would pretend he was invisible just so they didn't hurt his feelings.

"I am glad that is over." Eric sighed in relief. He had been watching the leaves and branches fall from the surrounding trees and cover him for the last one hundred years. Being frozen, he didn't really have a choice, but it was really annoying. As the spell started to wear off, the ice had started to melt, and the debris that covered him for the last one hundred years had started to slide to the floor. The glow from the newly exposed ice was what had attracted Owen.

"I knew it wasn't going to be long, but thanks for helping it on its way. I am starving." Eric hopped over to the big carrot, and stood in front of it for a second. He had been waiting one hundred years for this. He stood on his hind legs and leaned in for a big bite. Suddenly he felt a rush of pain from his ears to his toes as his teeth pinged against the still frozen carrot.

"Ow, ow, ow, ow!"

Ane laughed as Eric hopped around in pain. She took out her wand and created a little carrot for him. Owen noticed it happened straight away, again! Ane's magic never worked that easily. He could see the smile on her face, it was huge. Her magic was really kicking in and he was happy for her, concerned, but happy.

"Ah, that's sweet, but I like them a little bigger." Eric gave a twitch of his nose, and then another... and then another.

"That's odd? My magic must still be frozen?"

Ane looked over at Owen with a concerned expression; how was she going to tell one of the six that he had lost his magic? Owen, George, and Willow were almost next to them now; they had come a little closer to see Eric when he was hopping around. Ane waved her wand, and the carrot tripled in size. That made Eric happier. He took the carrot, and then sat on the ground next Ane. The others followed and sat with him.

"Eric, I have something to tell you about your magic…"

***

"I am not comfortable" Manuel was looking around him at all the people in the tavern.

They had all finished their dinner. There had been a vote to go to bed for an early night, but they couldn't do that before they had at least one supper. Well, maybe just two, and then they would go to bed.

"No, I am not happy. To be honest, they don't look happy either." David sat as close to the window as he could. While the others weren't looking he had opened it a little to check his chances of jumping out if the people in the tavern became hostile.

"Why do they keep staring at us?" Fred, like most wizards, was very good at stating the obvious.

"We are four of the greatest wizards in history, Fred. Why do you think they are staring at us? We have been missing for a hundred years and then, the day we turn up at their tavern, magic has disappeared from the kingdom. It is not hard to work out who they are going to blame for that?" It was The Horrible Hipolito turn at stating the obvious.

The table was silent.

"Who?"

They all looked at Manuel who instantly started looking at the floor.

"Excuse me…" Whilst looking at Manuel they didn't notice the waitress from the bar walk over to their table. The rest of the customers had been deciding for a while who was going to make the first approach.

"Yes, my dear?"

They all left it to The Horrible Hipolito to speak. Dealing with normal people wasn't something that wizards did well. They could deal with kings and queens as they knew they wanted something from them, but normal people were… well, normal.

"We were just wondering, all of us…" The waitress looked behind her. All the customers were nodding at her in agreement.

"Are you, you know, like wizards?"

The wizards looked at each other for a response.

"Like wizards? We are not like wizards my dear, we are wizards! We are The Four! The four most powerful wizards that ever lived!"

The waitress smiled, turned to her colleagues, and smiled again.

"Wow, that is amazing! We thought you maybe. Dan over there he said you maybe. I knew it was going to be good. I knew we weren't in any danger" She smiled back at all the rest of the people in the tavern.

"By the way, which one of you is The Great Burtoni?"

There was a groan from all four of them.

"None. None of us are The Great Burtoni. Why does everyone say that? We are the other four, you know, THE FOUR! Well, the other four, other than him and the rabbit. None of us are the damn rabbit, are we?"

The waitress quickly turned away, and went back to the people at the bar. The Horrible Hipolito sounded grumpy, and everyone knew that a grumpy wizard was never a person you wanted to be standing next to.

There was a lot of chatter. The mood seemed to change in the tavern. The Four Wizards just sat watching as the customers spoke amongst themselves. Five minutes later the biggest of the customers walked over to the table, and stood over them. He was a giant, a six-foot-seven giant now. He had noticed his new height when he got up that morning. He had hit his head on the door frame as he was heading to the bathroom, causing two stitches in his head. He was still a little grumpy about that.

"So, what did you do?" For a six-foot-seven giant he had a twenty-five-foot giant's voice. It was loud and booming it almost shook the table they were sitting at.

The rest of the bar fell silent. David was pushing the window a little more open with a view to climbing out of it.

"I am sorry, sir?" The Horrible Hipolito stood up to the giant. He placed one hand in his robe where the page was, to reassure himself. He still had magic. It was a little magic, simple, but he knew sometimes little and simple was all you needed with the normal people. After all, as he always said, people were little and simple.

"Magic is gone! We know that you did it!" He banged his fist on the table.

At that point David was already trying to get out of the window, unfortunately he soon realised that the window didn't open any further. His head was the only thing hanging out of the window. The whole bar started to buzz, and numerous comments started to fly around.

"Go on, Dan, hit him!"

"They deserve it!"

"Hit the big one" The wizards turned to look at Fred. He had tried to throw his voice to be one of the crowd with very little success.

The Horrible Hipolito stood up. The giant didn't move, but most people at the bar took a step back.

"I am not sure what you mean?" The Horrible Hipolito waved his wand.

The giant was lifted in the air, moved five feet back, and gently placed back down again. There was a stunned silence in the bar. All eyes were on The Horrible Hipolito.

"Magic is fine. A drink maybe, gentlemen, and lady of course? By way of a demonstration." The Horrible Hipolito then conjured up the glasses to come from behind the bar, they started to fill themselves with ale, and then landed on the table in front of all the stunned customers.

There was a silence. Nobody moved. Then, a minute later, there was a loud cheer. All the customers were cheering. The Horrible Hipolito sat back down. Normal people were so easy to deal with. Most of them wanted either food or drink. It was mainly drink if they were in a tavern. The Horrible Hipolito waved his wand again, and four further drinks landed on the table in front of them. There was another cheer from the on looking crowd.

"Think that should do it." Hipolito was looking proud of himself when he sat back down.

"If I had magic, I would have…"

They all looked at Fred who stopped speaking straight away. Even he knew not to finish the sentence.

***

"She will come here at some point Lizzy. She is a clever girl."

Ane's mother and grandfather were standing amongst the crowd in front of the palace. There were hundreds of worried people queuing to see the king and queen.

"It is what is written dad. I think it has started. It must have."

"It doesn't say when though, Lizzy, it may not be today. Besides, I am starting to think that she couldn't get here in a day? It is a long walk. Even for our Ane."

Ane's mother knew he had a point. It was a long way from their windmill to the palace.

"Do you suppose they are all here because of the book?"

"I would think so, Lizzy. They will all be wondering what has happened to Magic." They had both already worked out what had happened to magic in the kingdom.

It was why they were keen to find Ane, and as soon as possible.

"Are they what I think they are?" Ane's mother gave a confused look to her father.

"I think they maybe Lizzy."

There was almost a smile on Ane's mothers face as a gummy bear walked past her with a wheelbarrow full of soft drinks. He was selling them to the people in the queues. She knew that Ane had something to do with them, there were lots of them. She had flashes back to the kitchen sink not two days ago. They were red, red was her favourite colour, it was definitely something to do with Ane.

**

"I think, my dear, the best thing you can do is listen to them all, one by one. There are some concerns that something has happened in the kingdom? Apparently, things are changing, or so I have been told."

The king knew the queen knew more than she was saying. She always knew more than she said. He started fidgeting with his clothes not looking directly at his wife who was sitting in the throne next to him.

"I think I need to tell you something first, my queen."

The queen smiled at him.

"I already know, dear. I went to the Great Hall of Books. Something has happened to *The Great Big Book of Everything and Cheese and Onion Sandwiches*, hasn't it? And I am sure it has something to do with your new friend from last night. The one who, for some reason, came in a very, very bad disguise?"

"You knew it was a disguise?" The king knew it was. Looking back now, maybe that should have been a valid reason not to have listened to him. Actually, he was sure that he shouldn't have listened to him, but it was a little late for regrets now.

"Of course, it was. I did want to ask why. I thought it may have been a fancy-dress thing, although a really bad one. You seemed to get on well with him? You must have had a lot in common as you spoke to him for a long time.

The king thought back to how it must have looked. He was engaged with The Horrible Hipolito all evening. He had such interesting stories. Some he hadn't told Cook about yet, like the cold soup, cold tomato soup. It sounded wrong, but The Horrible Hipolito had made it sound so refreshing. Especially when you could put egg and ham in it too. Seeing the king that engaged with a subject of the court was something the queen would have not seen very often.

"The thing is, dear..." The King struggled getting the words out.

The queen could see how uncomfortable he was as he spoke. Through all his faults she loved the king. She loved him for who he was, and the fact that he had the interests of the whole kingdom at heart. She also knew he had a weakness though, and that weakness was his stomach.

"The thing is, he tricked you into doing something that you thought would benefit the whole kingdom.

Something that you thought would make everyone happier. Even happier than they already were."

The king listened and in return just nodded.

"Then, he tricked you into opening the book, and when you did, he removed magic from the book, didn't he? So, the spell that has ruled our kingdom for so long is now lifted."

The king nodded again.

She had guessed what had happened when the complaints had started coming in from the kingdom. It had helped seeing the word *magic* written with the king's handwriting on the first page of the book. The fact that it had also been written on every page thereafter had just helped to confirm it.

"He was probably a wizard, my dear, one of the greats. One of the Great Six. They are very powerful; I am sure they could have tricked anyone."

The queen pondered what she had just said for a moment. She had heard the chatter of their return from the crowd. They had been seen walking along the road but nobody was brave enough to talk to them. She knew it had been one hundred years too. It was then that the queen had her own lightbulb moment.

"I knew that I knew him… that I had seen him before, The Horrible Hipolito! It all makes sense now" She was almost shouting at this point, not that anyone but the king would have noticed. The king just nodded again at his wife.

The queen sat in silence. The king held his breath. He held his breath for as long as he could, then he breathed, and held his breath again.

"Okay. I need to go, my dear."

The king just looked at her, then looked at the crowd and then back to her again.

"But, darling?"

The queen was already up and ready to walk away. "Don't worry, dear, we will sort this out." She had that tone in her voice again. The one that told him she had this. She was in control of the situation.

"But, what do I do?"

The queen bent over, and kissed her husband on the cheek.

"Speak to the people, my dear, calm all their fears; be a king. Be a great king."

She disappeared out of the Great Hall. The king gave it a minute, and then beckoned the first person in the queue. He knew to do as he was told. The woman at the front of the queue was holding a pair of shoes. The toe of the shoes had been ripped open.

"It's my son, your Majesty, my son's feet have started growing. Not just his feet either, he is now seven foot six, seven foot six your majesty, and getting bigger every hour? What am I going to do, your Majesty? They don't make shoes any bigger? More than that, they don't make clothes any bigger. He is running around the palace gardens naked."

The king tried not to laugh at the thought of a giant child running around the garden naked.

"He is seventeen, Your Majesty. Seventeen-year-olds shouldn't be running around naked."

The king shook his head in agreement. When she had said son, he instantly thought she meant a little boy. The king looked for his wife again, but she had gone. It was up to him to tell this woman something.

"Seventeen, you say? No, he should not be running around naked at seventeen. I think we have a marquee out in the grounds, you can borrow that for the time being until we find you a tailor. A giant tailor."

Chapter 9

"No magic anywhere?" Eric had been saying that a lot as they continued to walk through the forest. Over the years he gotten used to using magic. For one, it had fed him for the last ten years. Well, the last ten years before being frozen for one hundred years, that was. There was nothing like a Giant Carrot for tea; he was going to miss that.

The fact that he was a rabbit that was still alive after one hundred and twelve years was also something he was thankful to magic for.

Ane had shared the whole story with Eric who was happy to help wherever he could. He was always happy to help; it is what had made him a Kingdom Treasure. Ane even told him about the day they had named after him after he disappeared. He loved the thought of that, especially the carrot hunt.

"Ane, it is getting late. Shouldn't we go... well, home?" Owen had never stayed out all night. Even when Ane had asked him to stay for a sleepover he always ended up going home. He always used the excuse that his mother was worried about him, and he didn't want his mother to worry. Ane knew the real reason but she never said it too him, she knew it was him who was really worried about being away from home.

"We are nearly there, Owen. We can stay at The Great Burtoni's house for the night, I am sure he won't mind. Then it is just a small walk to the palace tomorrow morning."

Owen wasn't sure about that. He knew when he left Ane's house there was a good chance that they were spending the night away from home due to the distance, but he didn't think it was going to be a night in the house of the greatest wizard of all time. He was happy that they would all be together though. Safety in numbers. That is what he kept repeating to himself in his head… there was safety in numbers. That, and the fact that Ane was probably scarier than anything they were going to meet in the woods was a comfort to him.

Besides, they had one of The Great Six with them now. People, or things, wouldn't attack them in the woods with one of The Great Six with them, even if he didn't have magic. They wouldn't know that, he was Eric, he was a legend. Owen convinced himself it was all going to be fine. No, he convinced himself it was going to be good; fine was Ane's word. He still couldn't shake the gummy bear selling sweets outside the school though, but as long as he didn't turn up everything would be fine… good, he was sure it would be good!

"I think this is it." Ane stood still.

About ten feet in front of her was a door that looked like it led into a tree. Branches had almost formed a porch area as you approached the door. The tree was huge; the biggest one at the edge of the forest. Ane could just about make out the size of a house at the back of it. She looked over to Eric who nodded his head. This was The Great Burtoni's house.

"Is it safe?"

Ane turned to Owen with a big smile on her face and nodded.

"Of course it is safe. He was The Great Burtoni. Nothing bad could come from here."

Owen wasn't so sure. The Great Burtoni was still a wizard, and not just any wizard, the most powerful wizard of all time.

Nobody else seemed really worried about it. Eric had visited The Great Burtoni lots of times. Out of The Great Six, they were the closest of friends. Eric always believed it was because neither of them wanted anything from the outside world.

Willow and George were engrossed in a game of I spy, and didn't really care either way. George had chosen "Tree" for the thirteenth time. Willow was trying hard not to guess it. It kept George laughing, and the sound of that had kept all their spirits up walking through the woods following Ane and Eric.

Ane walked up to the front door and knocked. There was no answer. She wasn't really expecting one. He had been missing for one hundred years. She didn't really expect him to be just sitting around at home for that long. She knocked on the door again. It moved. It was open! She gave it a little push, and the door opened very easily.

She looked down at the floor. There was dust everywhere, but the door looked like it had been moved recently, very recently. By the look of it, it could have even been today. All the post had been picked up from the floor, where she could still make out the letter shapes in the dust, then placed on the table. She could see the letters had moved the dust on the table too. Someone else had visited The Great Burtoni's house today; she was sure of it.

Ane walked in and they all followed. Owen was last, but he did follow.

"The Great Burtoni's house." Ane walked around as if she was in a daze. She had always wondered what a Great wizard's house looked like, smelled like. It smelled musty. That was how she would have expected it to smell, although secretly she expected more. She didn't let it show to the others though. There were more books than she thought there would be. Less beakers and less magic just hanging around in the air. She couldn't see one spell set up in the house. Her grandfather's basement was more impressive, well, maybe not at the moment as it was mid tornado, but generally it looked more magical.

"I am cold Ane."

Ane turned to Owen. She looked over at the fire and waved her wand at it. It lit instantly, everyone looked at her in amazement. Ane didn't give it a second thought. She just smiled to herself with acknowledgement that it had worked again. Her magic was well, magic today. Ane couldn't help thinking there was going to be some magic left in this house. If magic was remaining anywhere in the kingdom, it would be here.

"I will fetch some more wood before it gets dark Ane. I don't want to go out looking for wood in the dark." Owen beckoned over at George and left the cottage, slowly followed by Willow.

***

"Let's go back home and wait for Ane there? She may already be there waiting for us."

Ane's grandfather nodded his head. It was the right thing to do. The kingdom was large, and they had no way of knowing where Ane would be. Not without magic. He also knew they would be able to get back to the palace in a matter of seconds if they needed too.

"I think that sounds like a plan, my dear, and don't worry, Ane is a good kid, nothing is going to happen to her."

"But what if…?"

"What if? What if still means nothing bad is going to happen to her." There was a smile on her grandfather's face. It was small, but it was definitely a smile. What he was saying was partially true, Ane's mother knew that. If the prophecy was about to become true, Ane wasn't going to get hurt. Nothing bad was going to happen to her. Things were just going to change, and they both had the feeling that that had already started to happen.

***

"Do you remember the snakes? I loved snakes. Do we still have snakes?"

The ale had really been flowing; flowing and floating. The landlord didn't say anything to the wizards about helping themselves; after all they were four of the Great Wizards. He had tried to say it to the other customers though, but they pointed out that if the beer and wine were floating to them, it was not their fault. It was the will of the beer.

"I haven't seen any, besides, you remember what happened with the snakes, don't you, Manuel?" They all started to laugh.

Manuel just nodded. That had not been one of his better spells. It had involved sliding, wriggly snake like things... at the time he had been sure he had done the spell right, and they were going to be scary, but they hadn't been. He had ended up turning his army into worms! Half of his army of worms were then eaten by birds before he could change them back. His plan had been to terrify the army, and then sneak into the palace under the door before turning them back into soldiers. It had been a good plan, just not executed correctly. Manuel mumbled.

"If I had made snakes they would have taken care of your frogs."

The Horrible Hipolito heard what he said, and gave him the look. The look that said they were your frogs. Manuel's memory wasn't the best out of the four wizards either.

***

Eric stood over by the huge desk in the corner.

"He always loved his books. Doesn't look like he has been here for some time though. What happened to him?"

Ane walked over to the desk too.

"Nobody knows. When the other wizards, including yourself, disappeared, he disappeared too. When was the last time you saw him?"

Eric hopped onto The Great Burtoni's chair and started to spin around on it.

"Just afterwards. Just after *The Great Big Book of Everything*. I used to pop in and see him quite often when he was working on it. He told me it was a secret so I didn't say anything. The last time I came in here he asked me if he had done the right thing by restricting magic on the world."

Ane stood silent, thinking about that point. She was not sure what answer she would have given to that question.

"And what did you say?"

"I said yes. It was a good thing. Things were getting out of hand. The kings of each of the kingdoms were far too greedy, and wizards, well, The Four Great Wizards, which is what they called themselves in secret... maybe that is where you got The Great Six from ha ha ha that makes sense now... Anyway, the four wizards had lost the plot completely. They were turning people into anything and everything. We didn't get involved, but I do remember the battle of the unicorns though, it was the oddest thing I have ever seen."

"The battle of the unicorns?"

"Yes, unicorns. One night, after a late drinking session in a local tavern, they all decided to have a battle just with unicorns. The funny thing was that I think only Hipolito knew what a unicorn was. So, on the great battle field, the next day…" Eric had started to laugh.

"All four corners of the field were full with each of the wizards' armies. There were some unicorns, the Horrible Hipolito knew what he was doing, but there were also some other stranger-looking things. There were some yellow blobs that later turned out to be actual single pieces of corn. Manuel never lived that one down. He thought uni meant one piece. Neither did David though, he had an army of ears of corn. He figured that made him cleverer than Manuel. Fred on the other hand he was closer as odd as that sounds, he thought a unicorn was a horse with a horn… I must admit, the horn did help let everyone know when the battle started… diddly dee, diddly dee, diddly dee, dee, dee, dee." Eric was really laughing now.

"At least the real horses and unicorns didn't go home hungry." Eric kept laughing. Ane waited for him to stop, he looked like he was having so much fun.

"To be honest, the rules hardly affected me. I still had enough magic, which I mainly used to try to help people. Plus, without war, there wouldn't be as many people to cure anymore which left more time for carrots."

Ane was silent again. She loved magic. She loved everything about magic. Despite seeing what it had done to the world in history books she always wished there had been more magic. More magic everywhere.

"Wait, did you say *The Great Big Book of Everything*?"

"Yes, why?"

"Surely you mean *The Great Big Book of Everything and Cheese and Onion Sandwiches*? That's what it is called."

"It's called what?" Eric stopped spinning in his chair.

"That's what it is called? It has always been called that? *The Great Big Book of Everything and Cheese and Onion Sandwiches*. It's the book that rules our kingdom. It is the book that has everything in it."

Eric went completely silent. He looked stunned. Ane stood there looking at him for what seemed like ages. He then burst out laughing as hard as he could.

"What are you laughing at?"

Eric couldn't answer her. He was spinning and laughing at the same time now. Owen, George, and Willow walked into the Great Burtoni's house carrying firewood. Well, George and Owen were carrying the wood, Willow was more strolling around behind them.

"What is up with Eric?"

Ane shrugged her shoulders. "I don't know? He just started laughing, and I don't think he is going to stop."

***

"I luv… you. You are like the bests wizard I know."
Manuel was drunk, very drunk. The beer and the wine
had started to take its toll on all of them. The fact that he
was stood in front of the mirror talking to himself at the
bar didn't help.

"Hey, what did you say?"

Manuel turned around. There was a seven-foot-nine
giant bending down to talk to him.

"Huh?"

"You, pointy hat bloke, did you say you loved me?"

Manuel thought about it for a moment. He nodded
his head. He thought it was the best option.

The giant lifted him off the floor, without using
magic.

***

"I can't believe that she isn't home yet."

Ane's mother and grandfather were sat at the kitchen
table. The house sounded so quiet without Ane. They
were both thinking it. They expected her to run down the
stairs at any moment. Shortly followed by some kind of
crisis that needed fixing quickly.

"She will be fine, Lizzy. If she is not home tonight,
we will find her tomorrow, I promise. There is no point
us roaming the woods looking for her."

"I can't help but think?"

"There is nothing to think about. Nothing bad is
going to happen to her." There was a comfort in that

thought for both of them. Although if the prophecy was true, something was going to change her forever.

***

"Ane, what are we going to do about food?"

Ane had thought about that, but she hadn't figured on them all. She still had lunch and some treats from her secret stash, but she wasn't sure there was enough to go around.

"I have a sandwich."

Owen looked at her. Then looked around at how many of them there were.

"She has a sandwich, a sandwich..." Eric was still laughing so hard that there was the sound of something dropping on the floor behind him; it looked like a raisin. Eric didn't notice. Later that night Willow discovered, much to her disappointment, that it didn't taste like a raisin.

"I could just do this!" Ane put the sandwich in front of her, waved her wand over it, and it quadrupled in size.

Everyone's amazement continued, including Ane's.

"You are getting good at that!" Ane smiled. She was thinking exactly the same thing.

The friends sat and ate their dinner. Ane made the chocolate bars, biscuits and her bottle of orange pop quadruple in size too which continued to make everyone happy.

***

"Do you think that magic… you know, real magic, the thing with all the wands and that, do you think that it will come back?"

At this point the landlord had given up trying to be sensible, and had decided to join them all in drinking the floating free beer himself. He was sat in the booth with The Horrible Hipolito and Fearsome Fred. David and Manuel had been escorted upstairs to their room. Escorted was one way to describe it – they had been escorted through the ceiling of the tavern. The giant had managed to lift both of them through into their rooms from downstairs. The Horrible Hipolito had fixed the hole in the ceiling when the landlord had looked like he was going to cry.

"I think it will." Hipolito was comforting the landlord. He knew that landlords were the Kingdoms best use of gossip. That would keep the simple people happy. Knowing that magic was going to return. Magic, however small, had still played a key part of the Kingdom. For the last one hundred years, food was its main use. Witches and Wizards always came up with the best food, and quickly.

"When, when will it come back?" Fred wasn't being argumentative; he was just really drunk.

"Tomorrow, Fred, tomorrow will be our day." Fred nodded his head in agreement. Fred was happy to know that magic was returning. He missed magic.

They raised the glasses for another drink as they did it floated from behind the bar and filled their glasses. Even the landlord was smiling at that now.

***

Dinner was over, and now they were all cuddled up in front of the fire. Owen was laid next to Ane, he felt better laying there. George was a bit further away from the fire, just because he had started to sweat red liquid. Eric and Willow were cuddled up together too. They all felt cosy as they laid there.

"We can't go to sleep; we haven't had a bedtime story?" Ane looked at Owen. She had grown out of bedtime stories a long time ago. Clearly Owen hadn't. It didn't come as a surprise.

"What kind of story do you want?" Ane felt she had to ask the question, not that she knew many bedtime stories.

"Nothing too scary." That was pretty much a given from Owen. They all looked at each other to see who was going to tell the story. Finally, Eric spoke up.

"Do you know the story of Manuel and the queen bee?"

Everyone looked at Eric. They all shook their heads.

"Well, let's do that one then. Only Manuel could have ever got himself into that position." Eric loved telling wizard stories, and everyone always seemed to love listening to them. He would often visit villages and be paid in carrots for the good stories he told about the mishaps of his former colleagues.

"Okay, you may or may not know that sometimes over the past few hundred years Manuel has had one or two mishaps when it comes to magic. There was the time when he accidently turned his parents into goats. It was a long spell about kids which is a baby goat and it went amazingly wrong. He had a habit of sometimes shortening spells when they seemed too long. He believed that as long as most of the words were in there and in sort of the right order, then that would be okay and the spell would work."

Owen looked directly at Ane, and tried to raise one of his eyebrows, he was trying to give her the look, the look that said he knew she did that too. Ane just smiled at him. It was why she liked Manuel. The way he did magic always made a lot of sense to her.

"He also once recited a spell that made Fearsome Fred speak flowers. Every time, for two weeks, that Fred opened his mouth, a rose, or another type of flower, came out of it. All the other wizards, including myself, could understand why he wanted Fred to smell better, but again, it didn't really work. Anyway, this was a similar occurrence of Manuel, you know being Manuel." They all snuggled down ready for Eric's story. Each of them with a smile on their face in anticipation as they knew it was going to be a funny story.

"Early one morning Manuel decided to go for a camouflaged walk around the town. Being a self-proclaimed master of invisibility sometimes helped, but this wasn't one of those times. The spell hadn't worked; everyone could see him. To be honest, nine times out of ten they could see him. Manuel was likeable though, so people would pretend not to see him to spare his feelings, especially on days when he had forgotten to get dressed as well. Anyway, this was one of those days where he had forgotten to get dressed, and the spell hadn't worked. He stood next to a wall laughing to himself as people went past. He loved the way they always looked so happy in the morning. This in truth was mainly because they were struggling themselves not to laugh at Manuel pretending to hide, but he didn't know that.

"As he stood there a bumblebee landed on his arm. He did wonder how the bee knew he was there, but he figured bees were pretty clever. They made honey out of flowers so they had to be. This bee, however, wasn't very clever. He thought that Manuel was a big, very white flower. He wandered up and down Manuel's body looking for nectar. Manuel stood still as long as he could but started to get worried, especially as sometimes the bee wandered to places where bees shouldn't wander. So, Manuel recited a little spell to save himself from the bee. He knew the spell should have been a little longer, he even told me that. But, as always, he ran out of patience. Within seconds, the bee fell to the floor, but unfortunately so did Manuel. They were now eye to eye. The spell to remove the bee had turned out to be a spell to become a bee."

They all started laughing. This was the type of story everyone told about Manuel.

"Manuel turned himself into a bee! Initially he was shocked, especially when he came face-to-face with the other bee, but the other bee just smiled and flew away. Manuel thought about that for a minute, then realised that he could fly. He had always wanted to fly. Now, there he was, he just had to flap his wings and he was flying. This was going to be great. He quickly followed the other bee, figuring that if he was going to be a bee, he needed to know what a bee actually did. Manuel watched the bee as he headed towards the park and started to hop from flower to flower picking up golden yellow little sacks which he presumed correctly to be pollen. Manuel started to do the same, it was easy. He collected as much as he could, and followed the bee all the way back to his hive high up in a tall oak tree.

"When they arrived at the hive, they had to stand in a queue with dozens of other bees. Manuel was glad of the fact they had more than one pair of arms, the pollen was heavy. Unfortunately, they were on a royal inspection day. The queen had decided she wanted to see everything coming into the hive that day. It took a while, but finally it was Manuel's turn to present to the queen bee."

Eric stood up, well, as much as a rabbit could stand up, and tried to speak in a queenly-type voice.

"'Wait, you are not one of my children.' The whole room froze. Everyone had turned to look at Manuel, and then back at the queen. She was a big queen, about three times the size of every other bee. Manuel was scared, but it wasn't the first time he had been scared in the presence of royalty. He placed the pollen down in front of the queen. She wasn't the first queen he had met, and in those days, he knew how to deal with a queen.

"'No, Your Majesty, I am not, but I heard of your beauty from so far that I had to come and see it for myself.'"

Ane wondered if that was really what Manuel sounded like. It was sweeter than she imagined.

"There were mumblings from the other bees, more of a humming than a mumbling. Some of them were shouting *One of the nine! One of the nine!* Meaning, he was one of the nine major families that ran the bee world, but the queen didn't take any notice. She had taken a shine to Manuel, flattery was always the way to deal with a queen. The queen decided to clear the room and sent all the other bee's away. Manuel never speaks about what happened over the next few hours. I like to think that they sat and drank honey while talking about the weather. Anyway, after their morning of honey-drinking, Manuel went back out. He was that impressed with the queen and the life of a bee, that he decided to go and get some more pollen. An hour later he managed to find himself back at the hive. He landed as before, but this time there was no queue. He thought this was great and proceeded proudly to walk directly to see the queen. On his way, he could hear chants: *Honey... Honey.* Manuel didn't pay too much attention, figuring it was the worker bees having their lunch. He walked up to the royal chamber, strolled right in, and dropped the pollen in front of the queen. She wasn't alone though; there were guards everywhere.

Everyone turned to look at him. The room was stunned into silence until the queen shouted... 'HONEY!' Manuel bowed. *'Yes, sweetie, honey for my honey.'*

"Suddenly all the guards rushed towards Manuel. Immediately his instinct kicked in. He knew he needed to run, which he did, he ran faster than he had ever run before, he was sure and thankful the wings were helping with this. Turns out that honey didn't mean honey; it meant honeybee, the sworn enemy of the bumblebee. They had been at war for generations. You see, bumblebees collect all their pollen in the morning and honeybees work in the afternoon. So they never get into a fight whilst at work.

"The bees continued to chase Manuel through the hive, twisting and turning at every opportunity. Manuel was running for his life. Then he remembered he was a wizard, not a bee! A quick mumble of a spell and *BOOM!* He was himself again. Unfortunately, he had not thought the whole situation through. In hindsight, he should have done the spell outside of the hive. As soon as he became himself, he, and the hive, came crashing to the floor. The bees were stunned. There, sat in front of them, was Manuel, still naked, covered in honey. Suddenly Manuel heard a lot of buzzing, he quickly realised he could no longer speak bee. While Manuel is not very smart, it didn't take a genius to realise what the buzzing what saying, *Honey Bee and Get him.* Manuel picked himself off the ground and ran as fast as he could without looking behind him, and soon he was at the other side of Devil's Dip park. To the other people in the park, seeing a naked

Manuel wasn't a new sight, but seeing a naked Manuel covered in honey being chased by a swarm of bees was a new twist to his portfolio.

"Manuel knew he couldn't outrun them forever; wizards aren't very fit. He also knew that he wouldn't make it home. Then an idea popped into his head. Fred's house was just around the corner, he would get help there. The bees were getting closer and closer. By the time he got to Fred's front door they were practically on his shoulder. Manuel ran through the house until he saw Fred who was at the bottom of his garden. Manuel wasn't going to make it; they were definitely going to catch him. He kept running towards Fred while chanting his invisibility spell. Fred was busy with his own experiments on roses which he had become quite fond of since the flower incident, so he didn't see Manuel running towards him... or the swarm of bees. Ten feet before he reached Fred, Manuel tripped and, for once, the invisibility spell he had been chanting worked the moment he hit the ground."

At this point Ane had worked out the ending to the story, and was already smiling to herself. All the others were sat bolt upright waiting to know what happened with the bees.

"You see, bees follow their noses and, while we all don't smell the same, wizards sometimes, okay lots of the time, do. Their diet was very similar. Lots of food, followed by lots of ale, and then some more food. Fred heard the buzzing sound about five seconds too late to do anything about it. After the first fifty stings, he tried to run away, but as he was running he tripped over something. He looked everywhere, but couldn't see anything to trip over. He was definitely sure he had tripped over something though. Another one hundred and fifty stings later he managed to recite a spell which froze the bees. It took him six months to feel safe enough to go back into his garden, he was that afraid of bumping into a bumblebee. I don't even think Manuel has ever told him that story, although I know he told the others. They still make the buzzing sound around Fred when he gets too annoying. Just to scare him."

They all applauded, and Eric took a bow. It was a good story. Twenty minutes later they were all curled up by the fire fast asleep. All except George who was a little bit further away.

Chapter 10

"My head hurts." Fred woke up in the bathroom of the tavern, not in the bath, but on the floor in the bathroom. They had taken him out of the bath after they gave him a good wash. The other customers had finally worked out where the smell was coming from, and had decided to do something about it. The other three wizards had shared the bedroom. They were already up, dressed, and had gone looking for him.

"I miss hangover cures."

Everyone looked at Manuel. For once though, they were all in agreement with him. Back in the good old days of magic, which they had spent most of the night talking about, a cure was a cure and, all too often, their best cure was for a clear head in the morning. They had made most of their money outside of deals with kings and queens with that cure. Ane's grandfather still sold that cure today in his weekend markets.

The Horrible Hipolito could have still raised the cure today, but he was too hungover to do it. They helped Fred up and waited for him to get dressed. As soon as he did, the three wizards all looked at each other. Half of the smell had returned instantly. They realised at this point they probably should have washed his clothes too. They all headed downstairs to the bar area. There were various bodies sprawled across the bar, some on the tables, others on the actual bar, and some even on the floor and under tables. The thanks to the floating beer, drunken customers had slept where they had fallen.

"That was a wild night." David wasn't wrong; they had drunk every last drink in the tavern, remembering the good times when magic really ruled the kingdom, over and over again. The Horrible Hipolito had continued through the evening to do a few magic tricks to ensure the rest of the tavern knew that magic was still alive and well. They were simple ones, but as Manuel had pointed out, they were simple folk. That comment managed to get him a punch on the nose from Dan the giant but he was too drunk to feel it.

"I think we should just go. It is not far to Burtoni's house." The Horrible Hipolito lied a little; it was still a good few hours at the pace they walked, but he knew they would have never moved if he said that.

"What, leave? Without at least one breakfast?"

Everyone looked at Manuel; his outburst was too loud for this time of the morning. It was true that wizards rarely missed a meal and they never missed breakfast, at least not the first one. The Horrible Hipolito grabbed the paper in his pocket, and bananas appeared in everyone's hand.

"Fruit? What are we supposed to do with fruit?"

"Isn't this what we throw at people when they have been bad? After being placed in the stocks. Even they don't eat what we throw."

The Horrible Hipolito gave them all the stare. This time they didn't budge though. Wizards didn't like fruit. You could mess with them about most things, but never with their food. With a wave of his wand, the bananas turned into giant sized sausages in their hands. The three hungry wizards all smiled at each other.

"Now, come on, today we have to get magic back into the Kingdom."

The four wizards left the tavern, biting into their sausages as they did.

***

"What are we looking for, Ane?"

Ane wasn't really sure. She kind of thought she would know once she saw it. He was the greatest wizard of all time if something had happened to magic, she was sure that the fix, if there was indeed a fix, would have been there at his house.

"Something magical, maybe a wand or a spell book? It may be as little as one little spell." Ane was now wishing that The Great Burtoni had left his wand behind. She started to imagine the magic she would have been able to do with that. A lot more fun than Fred's old shoe that she had in her backpack.

George held up a twig that he had brought in last night for the fire.

"Nice try, George, but let's keep looking."

Everyone did as they were told. They searched all the drawers, cupboards, under all the tables, and even the wardrobes.

"Ane."

Ane turned to see Owen standing in front of her with a book.

"Yes, Owen?" He handed her the book.

"What is a lion?"

Ane looked at the book, and read the title. The lion the witch and the wardrobe. She knew what a witch was and a wardrobe, but she had never heard of a lion before. The Great Burtoni had known exactly what a lion was; he had been chased by one once, and it still gave him nightmares. It wasn't a coincidence that it didn't make it into *The Great Book of Everything and Cheese and Onion Sandwiches*. Actually, if they had been in the tavern the night before, they would have heard The Horrible Hipolito tell the story of when he had turned himself into a lion just to scare the Great Burtoni.

"I don't know." Ane flicked through the book.

"There are no holes, Ane, in any of the books? They are all complete? It looks as if everything there ever was is back into the kingdom! Well, the words are here anyway."

Ane instantly knew that meant her theory had been correct, but it wasn't just magic; something had happened to the *Great Book of Everything and Cheese and Onion Sandwiches*. It was no longer controlling anything in their kingdom. Everything that had disappeared was now back. Ane tried hard but she could hide the huge smile on her face.

***

"So, my dear, how was it yesterday? How were the people?"

The king was at the table eating his breakfast. He had four sausage and peanut butter sandwiches. The queen smiled, at least his appetite had returned. That had to be a good sign.

"It was fine."

The queen kissed him on the cheek, and took a seat next to him.

"That's good to know, my dear, as I have just been outside for my morning walk and there is a queue outside today that goes all the way down to the fountain."

The king choked on his sausage.

"They are what?"

"Down by the fountain, my dear. I guess that they all want to talk to you about what has happened." The queen knew why there were there. She had already been out greeting them all, and had instructed Cook to start cooking four hundred sausages, and make lots of tea for their guests.

"But, my queen, I can only tell them the same thing. I am not sure I can do anything about it? I fear this is how it is going to be from now on."

The queen smiled at her king.

"Sometimes it is enough to just hear that, my dear. They are just worried about their kingdom. You are their king. That is who they look to in their hour of need."

"They are not the only ones who are worried."

The king and queen turned. They had heard the booming voice before they noticed the door opening.

"What have you done, Albert?"

The king and queen stared at each other in amazement when they saw who had just walked through the door. Long flowing robes and a big long beard. Neither of them had ever seen him in those robes before. The Kings first thought was that he looked like he was only missing a pointy hat and it would have been a very good costume. Eventually the king spoke up.

"Mr Harrison?"

***

"I don't think we are going to find anything magical in here, Ane?"

Ane was starting to believe that was true. She was so sure there was going to be something, she didn't want to give up. All of a sudden, she spotted a box on the big desk in the corner. It had been hidden by books, but with all the searching they had been moved enough for the box to stand out. It looked like it could contain something special. They all surrounded the desk before opening the box. Ane was holding her breath. She flicked the little latch and opened the box… it was empty! The all looked at the box in disappointment. It looked like it should have had a wand in it. Ane was now truly convinced they weren't the first people to arrive at The Great Burtoni's house. Someone else had been there before them, she could tell from the movement of the dust on the desk and on the floor on the way in yesterday. Maybe they already took everything magical? Maybe it was The Great Burtoni himself? Maybe he had returned and was the reason there was an issue with magic in the kingdom? Ane had started to believe, especially given the last twenty-four hours, that anything was possible now.

"I think you are right, there is nothing left here. Let's go." Ane picked up her backpack, and headed towards the door.

Everyone followed.

If Ane had paid more attention she would have seen four wizards jump behind a tree in front of her as she started opening the door. If she had been two minutes later leaving, they would all have been face-to-face with each other on the Great Burtoni's doorstep.

"Where are we going?"

"To the palace, Owen. If something is wrong with magic, then something is wrong with *The Great Big Book of Everything and Cheese and Onion Sandwiches.*"

Eric started laughing hysterically as soon as the words came out of her mouth. They all shook their heads this time. Every time they mentioned the book he couldn't contain his laughter. In Eric's mind, the name of the book brought back great memories of his old friend sitting at his desk with his books.

"Ane, we're hungry."

Ane took out her wand and waved it in the air. The friends all had bananas appear in their hands. Well, all the friends except for one, he had a carrot.

"Cool, fruit."

The friends all followed Ane as she led them out of the woods, and in the direction of the palace.

***

The four wizards came out of hiding when Ane was a safe enough distance in front of them.

"Did you see that?" The Horrible Hipolito stood watching Ane as she disappeared over the hill.

"Yes, I did. She has carrots. I like carrots."

The other wizards were nodding in agreement.

"Not that, you idiots!"

They stopped nodding and all gave Manuel the look.

"Sorry." Manuel looked back at the ground.

"Eric. He meant, did you see Eric! I like Eric. I am glad that he is ok." It was Fred's turn to get the look.

The Horrible Hipolito was now shaking his head in disapproval at them all.

"No, not Eric! We are here after one hundred years so it isn't that strange that he is here too, he had to be somewhere! What is up with you three today?"

The three wizards all looked down at the floor as if they had just been told off by their school teacher. Nothing was said for a few minutes. Fred thought about saying that they had only had two breakfasts and yet to have lunch. But he thought better of it.

"Was it the gummy bear?"

"For crying out loud, it was the magic! The magic! That little girl has magic."

The wizards just looked at each other and then back at The Horrible Hipolito.

"We are the only ones with magic, right?" He took out the page and showed it to the others.

They all nodded.

"So, how does that little girl have magic?"

There were blank looks from the wizards. Somebody was going to have to reply to him, but none of them wanted to. David eventually thought it was his turn. After being prodded in the back from the other two wizards.

"Maybe she found it in The Great Burtoni's house?"

"I don't know why I bother." The Horrible Hipolito stomped off into Burtoni's house.

The other three stayed exactly where they were, nodding at each other at David's answer. Hipolito reappeared a few minutes later. It had been a good suggestion. The Horrible Hipolito had been thinking the same thing, but he didn't want to give praise to David. If the little girl had magic, she must have got it from the house, and that meant that she was the only other person in the kingdom with magic. Magic that should rightly belong to him as he was the greatest wizard of all time.

"There is nothing in there. His wand and his magic bag are gone."

"She was carrying a wand and a back pack?" Fred looked very happy with himself after saying that.

Manuel and David took one step back, then Manuel leaped forward with a burst of confidence.

"I think we follow the little girl and her friends, and find out where she got the magic from. Maybe we could get some more?"

There was a stunned silence as Manuel waited for his answer. The Horrible Hipolito thought about shaking his head in disapproval. There wasn't going to be anymore magic, if magic was anywhere it was going to be in this house. There wasn't going to be anymore magic but he could take the little girls magic for himself.

"You heard him." The Horrible Hipolito led the way.

The three wizards were so much happier, not only did they think there could be more magic, but it wasn't often that the Horrible Hipolito agreed with their answers. The Horrible Hipolito only had one concern. The little girl in question looked too comfortable with her new found magic if that is what it was.

***

"Lizzy, look at the map." Ane's grandfather laid the map on the table. It showed the whole kingdom.

"Right, if she is going from here to the palace... Where is the one place that she would stop by?"

Ane's mother looked down at the map in desperation, she didn't want to show it, but she was now beginning to get really worried. She followed the trail with her eyes, then instantly she saw it,

"Burtoni's house! Why didn't we think of that last night? She must have known where it was. That is where she would have gone. She would never miss that opportunity." Ane's mother smiled.

Ane's grandfather rolled up the map, and they headed back to the basement. Spinning the dials on the trunk one more time to number 00000123, they waited for the clunks and clicks to stop and they stepped in and walked down the stairs.

***

"Mr Harrison, what are you doing here? There is a queue, you know. I will be with you as soon as we finish breakfast." The King tried to sound firm, but he found himself not being able to look at Mr Harrison in the eyes.

"Never mind the queue Albert, what have you done to the book?"

The king looked down at his breakfast. Teachers had the same tone of voice as parents, and somehow queens. That voice that lets you know that you are in trouble. The king didn't respond. Even the queen seemed taken aback a little by the school teacher standing in front of them.

"I think you need to tell him, dear. Something tells me Mr Harrison is here to help you."

The king took a moment, and looked at his wife. She was nodding her approval at him. He stood up and took one last look at his half-eaten breakfast. He wasn't going to get to finish this peanut butter and sausage sandwich either.

"I think it is better if I show you, Mr Harrison, I would welcome any help you can give me."

The king stood up and headed towards the Great Hall of Books followed by the queen and Mr Harrison.

***

"Ane?"

Ane had seen them too, trying to hide between trees and bushes, sometimes too small to cover them fully. She had not wanted to point it out to the others as she knew they would be afraid. The wizards were as good at following people as they were at putting on disguises.

"I know, Eric, I have seen them. I was just wondering what they were doing?"

Ane and Eric were walking a few paces in front of the others. The others couldn't hear everything that they were talking about..

"I think they are trying to follow us without being seen. They never were very good at hiding." Eric almost had a laugh in his voice as he said that.

"You mean, they are who I think they are? All four of them?"

"Yes, they are. Those four always travelled together. You can normally tell by the hats, or the smell. Even from here you can smell Fred, but mainly through their pointy hats. You know, I never really liked wearing a hat, I try it over and over again, but I couldn't get it over my ears, you see."

"Why are they following us, Eric?"

"Who knows? They are wizards, and wizards are strange people. Maybe they know you have magic? Maybe they are following me? Maybe it is because we have a real-life gummy bear? Or maybe they are just going to the same place we are, and they don't want to walk with us. With that smell trust me, they are doing us a favour keeping that far back."

George, Owen and Willow were now all within earshot as Ane and Eric had slowed down to talk, they had heard bits of the conversation. They all started looking around, but couldn't see anyone.

"Who's following us Ane? I can't see anyone?"

"The Great Wizards are Owen."

"The Four Great Wizards." Eric this time laughed as he spoke.

"They always called themselves the Four Great Wizards"

"It will be fine, Owen. They are probably just going to the palace like us."

Owen and George looked around again, but they still couldn't see anything. Ane just carried on walking. Then Owen spotted a bush, about one hundred feet behind them, which seemed to be growing four pointy hats out of the top of it. All of a sudden, one of the pointy hats jumped out of the bush. Owen could hear him shouting "A bee! A bee! Get it off me!" Owen had to smile. His mind raced straight back to the story of the night before; he knew who that was.

They all kept walking, not really acknowledging the presence of The Four Wizards behind them. Ane was secretly star-struck; all of her idols were coming to life. That was five of The Great Six, all within one hundred and fifty feet of her. She was now convinced that at some point The Great Burtoni was going to make an appearance.

***

Mr Harrison stood in front of *The Great Big Book of Everything and Cheese and Onion Sandwiches*. It had been a while since he had stood in front of *The Great Big Book of Everything and Cheese and Onion Sandwiches*.

"One hundred years, and it had never been opened. One hundred years, Albert! Did your father and grandfather not tell you? Didn't they tell you never to open the book unless it was life or death? Was it life or death, Albert? Tell me, was it life or death?"

The king stood firmly, looking directly at the floor. Mr Harrison had always called him Your Majesty or sire; he had never called him by his first name before.

"Tell me exactly what happened."

The king looked directly at Mr Harrison. He had spoken in that teacher's voice again. He then looked back at the floor; he knew he had to tell him the whole truth.

"It started at dinner… he made it all sound so lovely. It was almost magical." As soon as those words left his mouth the king realised what he said. They were almost magical, he should have picked up on that.

"What sounded lovely?"

Now he was going to have to tell Mr Harrison and the queen the truth. He still hadn't told her the whole reason why he had opened the book.

"The food." The king paused and glanced at the queen.

The queen simply smiled; she already knew it would be something related to food. The king lived for food. Plus, she had seen him sneaking around eating buttered peanut and sausage sandwiches which nobody in the kingdom had ever heard of before.

"So you opened the book to put food in?" Mr Harrison wasn't so forgiving.

"Food, Albert! Life or death? Were you starving? Please tell me you were starving, and there was no other food in the kingdom." Mr Harrison's face was really red; he was mad.

The king had never seen him mad before. He had been a regular visitor of the palace for as long as he could remember. He would often come with the school children, and always seemed to love the Great Hall of Books. The king had always thought he was a very quiet man, a little odd, but shy and placid. In all the years, he could count with one hand the times they had actually spoken. Now he was seeing a completely different side to him, one which he was a little frightened of.

"I just thought that he had missed something. I thought that if there was something that the people liked in the past, maybe they would like to have it back. Give the people something different? You know, there is never anything different."

Mr Harrison just stared at him.

"What do you mean, missed something? Who do you think actually missed something?"

"You know, The Great Burtoni, maybe he missed some things when he made *The Great Big Book of everything and Cheese and Onion Sandwiches*."

"I, he didn't miss anything, Albert! The things he left out were on purpose. He didn't miss anything, all right!"

The king took a few steps back. There was a tone to Mr Harrison's voice that told him not to push that topic any further. The Great Burtoni didn't miss anything, and that was clear. There was a silence. Mr Harrison just stared at the book. Neither the king nor the queen wanted to interrupt his thought process. Then Mr Harrison stopped examining the book, and looked up at both of them.

"So, who was it? This person that tricked you into opening the book, who was it?"

"I think it was one of them, sir, one of The Great Six. At first I thought it was The Great Burtoni himself, but it turned out it was The Horrible Hipolito." The King immediately noticed the look of disgust on Mr Harrisons face at that revelation.

"They hardly look the same, Albert! The Great Burtoni hardly resembles a little butterball turkey with a big bushy moustache."

The king looked warily at Mr Harrison. That was an odd thing to say, let alone to be so upset about it.

"Well, he was wearing a disguise," the king answered a little sheepishly.

The mad expression on Mr Harrison's face started to change. There was almost a smile sneaking out of the corner of his mouth now. However mad he was with the king, he did like him. He wasn't a bad king; he was simply a good king. Everyone knew that. Mr Harrison looked back at the book.

"Has it really been a hundred years already?"

The king and queen looked at each other.

"Pardon?"

Mr Harrison didn't respond. He just continued looking at the book. He opened it again and went through it, page by page. The king and queen remained silent until he finished.

"So, he took the page of magic? Anything else? Has anything else been changed?"

"Yes, I mean, no. He took the page, yes, and no, he didn't do anything else." The king was waffling a little. "Wait, he said something about the binder, and sewing the pages in. He said The Great Burtoni hadn't thought of that. Hadn't thought about protecting that. That is why he could do what he did."

Mr Harrison didn't say anything. Nobody did for a good few minutes. It took the queen to break the silence.

"Can you fix it? You know back to the way it was before?"

The king gave his wife a stunned stare while mouthing the word "HIM?" to her. He couldn't understand why she would ask that question. There was silence again.

"No. All the magic in the kingdom was bound into that page. If I had the page, we could do something, but without it, I just can't. The only person that has magic in the entire kingdom now is The Horrible Hipolito. I just hope he doesn't realise how much magic he has."

Chapter 11

"She is not here?" Ane's mother walked around The Great Burtoni's house sweeping every room in detail. It was not her first visit to his house.

"No, she is not, but she was here." Her grandfather picked up a large chocolate wrapper. Ane's mother smiled and part of her relaxed. She knew that was Ane's favourite, and the one she had packed for her lunch the previous morning. Although it had quadrupled in size.

"And look at the floor, I can see evidence of where someone has been laying by the fire, maybe two people. One is small enough to be an elf. Over here, maybe a cat." There was a pause as they both looked at the shape next to the car. "And what looks like a rabbit?"

They both fell silent and stared at each other. They knew who that was. Eric had been missing for a long as *The Great Big Book of Everything and Cheese and Onion Sandwiches* had been written.

Ane's mother broke the silence.

"Then it is true. It is all coming true. Now that Eric has returned as well, everything is starting to link together. The prophecy states that they all need to witness it when it happens."

Ane's grandfather gave a small nod. He didn't really know what to say. He could see she was starting to get upset again.

"I read the poem again last night just to check. Just to check if something wasn't aligned." Ane's mother pulled a piece of paper out of her pocket and placed in on the Great Burtoni's desk.

"The ice will melt and the land will turn red.

The words once forgotten will return to your head.

Hidden from the kingdom, are the lands of our past

All will become visible as the last ever wizard spell is cast."

Ane's grandfather walked over and gave her mother a hug.

"Don't trouble yourself with it Lizzy. Come on, put the rest of the poem away. We have time to be there, besides the land hasn't turned red? Not that I have noticed. Let's go and find our little Ane." He turned and led her back up the stairs that had magically appeared in the corner of the room ten minutes ago.

The door disappeared behind them.

***

"Ane, don't you think that we need to get into the queue? It is the polite thing to do. They are handing out sausages and everything. I think I saw some tea as well?" Owen started to worry as Ane kept walking towards the palace doors, bypassing the queue. He knew she wasn't one to follow rules, but everyone was looking at them.

"It will be fine, Owen, the king and queen will want to see me. Besides, these people are here to ask what is wrong with the kingdom, and we already know that part. We just want to fix it." Ane carried on walking with the four friends following closely behind.

Willow and George each took a sausage as they passed Cook handing them out... Cook didn't look happy, trying to feed the hundreds of people as they were waiting to see the king, and she was sure that gummy bears were stealing her sausages when she wasn't looking.

"Ane?" Owen ran to catch up with her.

"I see them, Owen." Ane was determined to get to the palace, and nothing was going to distract her from that.

"Not the wizards, Ane, I was going to say have you seen..."

"No, I know what you meant, Owen. They are fine, they are not doing anyone any harm."

Owen was pointing out that nearly every third person in the queue was a gummy bear, a red gummy bear. None of the gummy bears that were in the queue knew why they were in the queue; they just saw it and joined it. To be fair, it wasn't just the gummy bears, there were some others in the queue that had done exactly the same thing too. The general feeling was that if there was such a long queue, there must be something good at the end of it.

Owen was now frantically looking around to see if any of them were selling bags of sweeties.

"Ane, it is like a sea of red out here."

Ane didn't take any notice. She was too focused on the palace.

None of the gummy bears were selling sweets, he was sure of it. There were lots of people with their phones at the end of a long pole taking photos with the gummy bears though. Also, on the sides of the queue there were what Owen believed to be gummy bear street sellers yelling, "*Selfie sticks, selfie sticks...*" The friends just looked at each other and shrugged their shoulders. The centre of the kingdom seemed like a strange place, and it was a lot busier than they had expected.

"Ane?" It was Eric's turn to catch up with Ane.

"I can see them too, Eric. They have been less than two hundred feet behind us all the way. You were right, I think they were just coming to the palace."

Eric just nodded and continued to hop next to Ane. Owen was starting to wonder if Ane had some sort of spell working. For some reason, she could see everything that was going on. She was in control of the whole situation without the support of her mother and grandfather. That wasn't like Ane.

In the last twenty-four hours, she had been focused, and good with magic. That was also unlike Ane. It wasn't just the fact that she had her grandfather's wand; it was something different. She was taking responsibility. Owen was secretly proud of that; he had been slowly educating her to do that. He was now sure at least some of what was happening was his doing.

Ane and her friends arrived at the palace doors. There were two big guards stood to attention right in front of them, none of which took the time to even glance in their direction. It seemed nobody was allowed in yet. The queen had told the guards she would let them know when they were allowed to open the doors.

"I want to see the king." Ane was looking directly at them when she spoke.

The guards didn't move. They didn't even look down.

"We want to see the king."

The guard looked down at the rabbit. He then looked over to the other guard and raised an eyebrow. A talking rabbit wasn't something you saw every day. Eric nodded at Ane. She levitated both of them in the air for about thirty seconds, and then slowly put them back down again.

The guards started to feel uneasy. They knew something was going on in the kingdom; something related to the disappearance of magic. It had been the topic of conversation of all the visitors yesterday. That, coupled with a little witch and a talking bunny... a bunny that could quite easily be...

"The name is Eric, and we want to see the king." Eric nodded at Ane again, and she replaced each of the guards spears with a banana with a single wave of her wand.

One of the guards started shaking. He didn't like where this conversation was going. This was way above their job description. For years, being a guard in the castle had just meant an orderly line with polite visitors, mainly children admiring the castle. They were not used to confrontation. Plus, everyone had heard of the powers of The Great Six and, although Eric was supposed to be the nice one, they didn't want to try their luck. They immediately opened the doors and let them in, closing the doors behind them.

"That was easy."

They all nodded at Eric.

"We need to go to The Great Hall of Books."

Ane led the way and marched her friends directly to the hall. She knew the way like the back of her hand; she loved this room just as much as her favourite teacher had. As they got closer, they started to hear voices coming from inside the room, one of which sounded strangely familiar. Ane pushed the door open, and for the third time in two days she found herself lost for words… she wasn't quite ready for what was waiting for her on the other side. It took a while, but the name finally came out of her mouth.

"Mr Harrison?"

The king, queen, and Mr Harrison, who were all standing around the book, turned to look at her, their faces reflecting as much surprise as the rest of the visitors that were walking through the door. Well, all of them except George and Willow who were just happy still munching on their sausages.

***

"She didn't queue? She went straight up to the door and they let her in?" Manuel was standing at the back of the queue.

"I know it's the polite thing to do, but we don't have time. That girl has magic, and we don't know how much she has. We need to follow her!" The Horrible Hipolito started to walk past the queue towards the palace.

"Back to the scene of the crime though? Won't the guards recognise you?"

The Horrible Hipolito shook his head.

"No, I wore a disguise. Besides, we have the magic now. What are we to be worried about?"

The four wizards walked up to the gates, The Horrible Hipolito still unsure of what he was going to say. Fortunately for them though, they didn't have to say anything to the guards. As soon as they got to the door, the guards just opened the door, and then closed it again once they were inside. The hats were enough of an invite for the guards. Whatever was going on inside that castle was going on inside, and they were outside. Surely it was safer being outside. Anyway, it probably had something to do with magic, so they figured magicians must be invited. They were doing the king and queen a favour by not delaying their meetings.

***

"Mr Harrison?" Ane repeated to herself. He was the one person she really didn't expect to see there, or did she?

"Ane? What are you doing here?"

Ane just stood looking at her teacher in amazement. There was something about him, something she hadn't seen before. Her mind was working overtime, there was something trying to surface. It was almost as if she wasn't surprised to see him standing in front of *The Great Book of Everything and Cheese and Onion Sandwiches*.

"Cheese and Onion Sandwiches!"

They all turned to Eric as he started laughing again, repeating the words to himself. Mr Harrison looked at him, and shook his head with a slight grin appearing in the corner of his mouth. Ane glanced at both of them; it felt like a private joke. Why would her teacher and Eric have a private joke?

"Ane, what are you doing here?"

Ane turned around to look at Mr Harrison again. He had his teacher's voice on.

"I came to help. Something is wrong with magic sir."

The king and queen were looking directly at her. Something in her voice sounded as if she was convinced she could actually help.

"But, you can't help, Ane. This is grown-up business. You and your little friends need to go home. Your mother, Lizzy, will be worried."

"But, Mr Harrison." Ane reached for her wand.

"No buts, Ane, run along now. It is time to go home."

That tone of voice was one she knew all too well. It meant *don't say anything else, Ane, and go home.* Ane turned to go, but as she did, something came into her head. Mr Harrison has used her mom's name, Lizzy.

With far too much familiarity. He had never done that before, he had always called parents by their full name. Teachers always said Mr or Miss.

Her thoughts were quickly interrupted as the doors behind her burst opened again. The four pointy hats that had been following her through her journey came into the room.

"Mwah, mwah, mwah!"

Everyone stopped and looked at Fred.

"What? I thought it was an evil laughter moment?"

The Horrible Hipolito just shook his head.

"What did we say, Fred? Leave the thinking and doing to me, and the laughter… I do the evil laugh; it is my thing." The Horrible Hipolito turned back to the room.

"Mwah, mwah, mwah!" The Horrible Hipolito turned to Fred as if to say *That is how you are supposed to laugh.*

Neither laugh scared anyone in the room.

"Now, listen here, I won't be tricked again. Do the right thing, and put the page back into the book like a good chap." The king was already walking over towards the wizards as he said that. He wanted to ensure he looked brave in front of his queen, but deep down inside he was shivering at the thought of how silly they could make him look in front of her.

"Not you again, I thought you would have eaten yourself into a slumber by now."

The king started to levitate again. That was exactly what he had started to fear.

"Hey, this is not nice! Now, put me down, I order you, I am a king!" The king was trying to remain brave even when he was five feet off the ground.

Ane took off her backpack and opened it. If this was going to come down to magic, then she was going to need all the magic she had.

"Put him down, Hipolito." Mr Harrison spoke with an even more booming voice.

Ane thought she had heard him cross before, but nothing like this. The king was lowered safely to the ground.

"Now, hand it back please!" Mr Harrison said with a stern voice.

Fred, Manuel, and David took a step back from Hipolito. The Horrible Hipolito took the page out of his jacket, and started walking over towards Mr Harrison looking like a school kid who had just been told off. Then, as if he had just realised something, he stopped midway across the room.

"Wait a minute, did you say hand it back please? Hand it back please? You are never that polite? You don't have it, do you? Even you... you would never ask so politely. You would just have taken it back. It's not like you. You don't have any magic, do you?"

There was silence.

"Mr Harri... son!!" Owen shouted out.

The whole room stopped to look at Owen, then quickly turned their attention to Ane as Owen was looking directly at her. She shook her head from side to side. Owen's outburst was as much a shock to her as it was to anyone else.

"Ane, listen to what I am saying... Mr Harry's ... son."

Ane didn't have to think for long. She got what Owen was saying straight away. When you are best friends it only takes a few words to express your thoughts. It all came back to her straight away. She remembered everything she had read back in the history block. She remembered his parents' name; his father's name... Harrold, Harry... he was Harry's son!

"Mr Harrison... you are The Great Burtoni?"

The whole room was now looking at her. Ane felt like she had revealed a big secret. Of course, the wizards, and Eric, already knew who he was, and the queen had also figured it out ages ago. The king was the only person to be surprised. George and Willow were also surprised, but they didn't know who either Mr Harrison or The Great Burtoni were.

"He is? You are The Great Burtoni?" The King asked.

The whole room waited in anticipation for the answer. Mr Harrison gave a nod toward the king.

"Yes, yes, he is, but he doesn't have any, do you? You didn't even keep magic for yourself? Only you would do that, only you would be that righteous."

The Great Burtoni, formally known as Mr Harrison, didn't agree or disagree with the statement. He stood still in front of *The Great Big Book of Everything and Cheese and Onion Sandwiches*.

The Horrible Hipolito took out his wand and held the page of magic in the same hand.

"Don't." The Great Burtoni meant what he said and everyone heard it.

Ane emptied her bag in front of her. Owen, George, and Willow took a step back. The Horrible Hipolito looked at the other wizards smiling as The Great Burtoni started to lift off his feet. There was a chuckle from the other wizards, but only very softly. The Horrible Hipolito spun The Great Burtoni over his head.

"Put him down!" Ane shouted. She had her grandfather's wand out in front of her.

"Wait, is that my shoe?"

Everyone, except Ane, looked at Fred who was pointing at the shoe in front of Ane. He couldn't remember where he had lost it. He had woken up with a big bruise on his head that day, but it was definitely his shoe.

The Horrible Hipolito lifted off the ground.

"Don't just stand there! Get her, you idiots!"

The other three wizards ran towards Ane. Ane ran towards where The Great Burtoni was floating.

Eric and George stayed behind and tried holding the wizards back. They weren't much use, but it was good to see that George could bounce. He was never going to get hurt by people running at him at full pelt. He bounced almost higher that the Great Burtoni. Ane ran over to *The Great Big Book of Everything and Cheese and Onion Sandwiches*.

"Mr Harrison, what do I do?"

Mr Harrison reached into his pocket, and took out his wand. He didn't say anything; he just threw it down at Ane. Unfortunately, wizards weren't known for their athletic skills, not even the greatest wizard of all time, and the wand ended up ten feet away from Ane.

"Get the wand, you idiots!" The Horrible Hipolito shouted at the rest of the Great Four.

The wizards changed direction and started running towards the wand. Then, out of nowhere, Owen appeared. He leaped across the rail, ran, and picked up the wand. It was the bravest thing that Ane had ever seen Owen do. She was so impressed. Owen had even surprised himself. He ran towards Ane as fast as he could.

"What do I do with it?" Ane questioned.

Mr Harrison didn't say anything. He knew if he did, then everyone would know what would happen; they would be prepared. He trusted Ane would know what she needed to do next.

In the great hall of books before all their eyes
The last ever witch will begin to rise

Mr Harrison recited the poem to himself in his head, he was the only person in the room that knew the prophecy. Deep down he knew it was always going to happen, and after teaching Ane for the last few years he had always been ninety nine percent sure it was going to be her that fulfilled it.

It was up to Ane what she did with the wand now. Mr Harrison just knew that the wand needed to be protected, and Ane was the only person in the room willing to protect it. Owen got to Ane, and handed her the wand. She now had two wands. She held them both out in front of her. The other three wizards froze.

"Get back!" Ane shouted at the wizards as loud as she could.

The wizards took three paces back; David took four, just to be safe.

"Get her, you idiots!"

They all looked up to the Horrible Hipolito who was still floating above them with Mr Harrison.

"But, she has magic!" Manuel spoke with authority for the first time. It was hard to disagree with him.

"Let Mr Harrison down, and I will let you down." Ane was looking directly at The Horrible Hipolito.

The Horrible Hipolito thought about it for a moment and then did as he was told. Not because he wanted to, but because floating around was starting to make him feel sick.

Once everyone was firmly on the ground, The Horrible Hipolito and Ane stood looking at each other. They were the only two people in the room who had magic. The Horrible Hipolito had the page, and Ane had her wand, well, she had two wands. Somewhere in the back of The Horrible Hipolito's mind, there was a doubt that he didn't have enough magic to take on the little girl.

He knew his magic was restricted, and Ane had the wand of The Great Burtoni. But then, a second thought entered his mind, she had only just got the wand of The Great Burtoni. That meant that his initial theory had been wrong, she had magic before she got the wand.

Neither Ane nor The Horrible Hipolito knew for sure if The Great Burtoni's wand could do any magic. All they knew was that The Great Burtoni didn't have any magic, so how much use would his wand be?

"Answer me this, little girl, how do you have magic?"

Ane didn't answer him. She thought it would be better if he didn't know too much. She did smile to herself though, she was happy with how her magic was performing. It had never worked this well. Ane was becoming a better witch. She questioned if it was only because she had her grandfather's wand, but that was something to worry about later.

"It is powerful, isn't it, the call of magic." The Horrible Hipolito had a plan forming in his head. All young people loved magic, surely that was the reason she was here.

"Can you imagine a kingdom without rules? A magic kingdom without rules? We can create that, you and I, we have the power."

Ane was looking directly at Mr Harrison who was shaking his head.

"Imagine all the magic tricks, all the spells you ever wanted. They could all be yours, little girl."

Ane looked at her friends. They were all looking straight at her; it was as if the whole room had frozen. Well, not the whole room, everyone had been so focused on Ane and the Horrible Hipolito that nobody had seen Fred sneak up behind Ane. He grabbed the wand from Ane's hand, and ran. He had it, he had the wand! Initially, the thought of keeping it crossed his mind, but then he remembered he couldn't use it, and threw it directly at Hipolito. The throw was another poor one. It had managed to travel half the distance it needed too.

"GET IT!"

Everyone dived towards the wand. The Horrible Hipolito got to it first, and immediately everyone else backed off and froze again.

"Mwah, mwah, mwah!" The Horrible Hipolito gave his laugh again. He was holding both wands in his hand. "See, Fred, that's the time to use the evil bad guy laugh. Now, I have your wand and the page... you know what, I have also just figured out what your backup plan is! I know you... you would have never left magic open like that. You always have a backup plan. Pigs in blankets, am I right? They were always your favourite weren't they? Well your second favourite next to... Holy Moly now I get it."

They all turned to look at Mr Harrison. He tried his hardest not to make an expression, but wizards were not good at hiding their feelings.

At that point, there wasn't anyone in the room that thought that The Horrible Hipolito had been incorrect with his statement. He had the magic page, and now he had the key to open it. He took the page, wrapped it around the wand, and held it high in the air.

"Mwah, mwah, mwah! Pigs in blankets."

Nothing happened. He held it up again, but again nothing happened.

"I don't get it! I was convinced you would have used the old wrapping paper trick. It is one of your favourites."

Just as he lowered his hand, from out of nowhere, Willow jumped and caught the wand and the page in her mouth. She started running towards Ane like the room was on fire.

"Get the damn cat!" The Horrible Hipolito shouted at the other wizards.

Willow managed to get to Ane and give her everything before getting caught. Ane hurried, unwrapping the wand from the page. Fred had stolen the wrong wand; he had taken her grandfather's wand. She then imitated what the Horrible Hipolito had just done, but this time, with the real Great Burtoni's wand.

"No! Ane!" It was too late. Owen's words of advice were lost.

All of a sudden there were fireworks, a lot bigger fireworks than Ane had made in the classroom; bigger fireworks than any of them had ever seen indoors. Thankfully, they were magic fireworks and nobody had to worry about setting The Great Hall of Books on fire. Ane started to rise off the ground and slowly spin in a circle. At the same time everyone else in the room started backing away from her – everyone except Mr Harrison. Mr Harrison stood up and walked towards her. Ane was spinning around in what looked like a firework herself. She was mesmerised in what was happening around her. It made her feel happy and excited, but a little scared at the same time. She loved that feeling. Then as the fireworks started to die down, the page that was wrapped around the wand crumbled away to dust, and Ane slowly fell towards the ground.

Mr Harrison was there to catch her. George gave a little round of applause. This was definitely the best show he had ever seen.

George, Owen, Willow, and Eric slowly headed over towards Mr Harrison and Ane.

"What happened?" Owen was standing the closest to Mr Harrison.

"She will be fine, Owen, probably a little dazed from the fireworks."

Ane dropped the wand on the floor. Mr Harrison didn't notice. He just carried Ane over to the step and sat her on it. She felt a little groggy from the spinning around, but she also felt as if something had just changed within her. She couldn't put her finger on it, but she felt different.

"Are you okay, Ane?"

"I think so, Mr Harrison. What happened? I feel a little weird."

"It is a very, very long story, Ane. You see, there is a prophecy; a prophecy I think you were born to fulfil. This is just the beginning of... "

"Mwah, mwah, mwah!" It was the third evil laugh they had heard in less than ten minutes. This time it was Manuel. It really didn't sound evil; it was more of a slightly baddy laugh with a hint of a giggle. He had the wand that Ane had dropped in his hand.

"Now I have the power." He pointed the wand at Mr Harrison and Ane.

Mr Harrison just turned his attention back to Ane.

"Did you hear me? I have the power! I am the most powerful wizard in the kingdom. At last, I knew I always would be. It is the time of Manuel. Mwah mwah mwah"

"Yes, I heard you." Mr Harrison wasn't paying any attention.

"Be afraid, be very afraid!" Manuel shook the wand. Nothing happened. He shook it again. Nothing happened.

Fred ran over and grabbed the wand from Manuel's hand. They all looked at Fred. Manuel messing up magic was normal, but Fred was a better wizard. He wasn't a great wizard, just a little bit better than Manuel. Fred had a go. Again, nothing happened.

Mr Harrison turned his attention back to Ane again. "The prophecy, Ane, it speaks of The Last Witch, the last person to hold magic in our kingdom. Well kingdoms. It also speaks of lands that even I know nothing about." There was almost guilt in his voice at that point. There were some lands that were lost to the Kingdom *after the Great Big Book of Everything and Cheese and Onion Sandwiches*. The prophecy speaks of lands that none of the Wizards have ever visited. Well none of the Wizards present in the room today.

"You will have a lot to do, Ane."

"I am The Last Witch? The last ever witch?"

The Great Burtoni was nodding his head.

"There is a lot I need to tell you, Ane. I need to help you get prepared for what is to come." The Great Burtoni could tell that Ane was tired. This wasn't a conversation she was ready to have at the moment.

"But, that is not for now, there is time for all that. How are you feeling?"

"I am fine, sir. Sir, are you really The Great Burtoni?"

"I was, Ane. Well, I was a long time ago, now I am just Mr Harrison. I gave up the world of magic when I knew the kingdom was finally safe. Nobody needs that much power, Ane. It goes to people's heads."

The wizards were all taking the wand away from each other and trying to use it. Nothing was happening.

"I didn't know about the prophecy then. To be fair, I didn't know a lot of things. I wasn't as wise as I thought I was. It would seem the book, and all of this was just part of that bigger prophecy. If I had read more I would have known that." Ane now had visions of Mr Harrison at school. All the time he had spent with his head in a book had been on purpose. He wanted to ensure he knew more about the world than anyone else. Something he wished he had done before laying the book down.

"What have you done with the magic, Burtoni? Where has it gone?" The Horrible Hipolito was mad, and so were the others. There was no magic left in the wand, and the page was gone.

"Burtoni! Pay attention to us!" The wizards were all running towards Mr Harrison and Ane now.

Ane stood up, as if by instinct, and held out her hand. They all froze. Everyone looked at Ane in shock. Ane looked at her hand. She was more shocked than anyone else. She didn't even have a wand in her hand.

"I did that? I was just going to say *No, leave him alone*."

Everyone was still looking at Ane.

"That's what I was about to tell you, Ane. You are magic now, there is no more magic in the kingdom. Well, there is one more piece of magic, but that is long gone. Lost for hundreds of years. The prophecy tells us it is going to be you that needs to protect us once it is found again."

Ane was in shock. She was not the only one though, the rest of the room felt exactly the same.

"Protect you from what?" Ane said wearily. Mr Harrison paused and looked at his audience. He knew he had already said too much in front of them all.

"I think that is for another day, Ane. I think you may have had enough excitement for one day."

Ane sat back down in shock. It still hadn't settled in. Willow was the first to approach her. She came up jumped on her lap and licked her hand. Then cuddled up in Ane's lap.

"What about them?" Ane looked over to the four frozen wizards.

"They are just men now, Ane. They won't give you any nonsense. They have no powers."

There was a frozen mumble of agreement. Ane lifted her hand and un-froze them. They all fell to the floor.

"Thank you. Thank you so much. I couldn't bear the thought of another one hundred years of that again." Manuel was smiling at Ane.

The others were too. The thought of being frozen for another one hundred years was more than any of them could bear.

"I am hungry."

Everyone turned to look at George. The king was nodding his head in agreement, and you never had to ask a wizard more than once. Mr Harrison looked at Ane; he had just realised there was a talking gummy bear in the room.

"Oh, yes, George… it's another long story, sir."

The king led everyone, including the wizards, to the Great Feast Room. Ane had given Fred back his shoe; he was holding it, and stroking it like a puppy. He was sure that giving him back his shoe was a sign of a new great friendship. He was starting to think he was now the Great Ane's new favourite wizard. Wizard with no powers, but wizard nonetheless.

"I can just call Cook, she makes the most amazing peanut butter and sausage sandwiches. Have you ever tried them? They are amazing." The king sat at the head of the table while everyone else took their seats.

Mr Harrison looked over at Ane and winked.

"There is no need to call Cook, sire." Ane stood up and filled the table with food with a wave of the new wand she had inherited from Mr Harrison. It now only worked for her, so it was no longer any use to him. After a brief conversation with the king, Ane even managed to make peanut butter and sausage sandwiches for everyone.

"Very impressive, little lady." The King said.

Everyone started to tuck in to the feast that was laid in front of them.

"Mr Harrison?" The king handed over another peanut butter and sausage sandwich.

Mr Harrison declined it, and, out of nowhere, he took out his lunch box. He opened it, and took out a sandwich. Eric started to laugh hysterically again.

"Cheese and Onion Sandwiches... ha ha ha!" Eric was helpless again; he laughed so hard he fell off of the stool.

Mr Harrison started to feel everyone looking at him. He tried to ignore it, but after a few minutes he couldn't any more.

"Okay, okay... yes, Cheese and Onion Sandwiches, that was me. They are my favourite."

The room was in a stunned silence.

"I realised very, very suddenly that I may have forgotten a few things from the book. I guess I am going to have to tell you the story now. I was giving Albert's grandfather a lecture about not opening the book. I was so serious at the time that I think it made him cry a little. After I calmed him down, we decided to have a second lunch, and it was then that I suddenly realised that I couldn't make my favourite lunch. I had forgotten to put it in the book. I couldn't then, in front of Albert's grandfather, open the book and write it in; it wasn't a matter of life and death. So, I just scribbled it on the front of the book. That is why it was called *The Great Big Book of Everything and Cheese and Onion Sandwiches*."

There was a moment's silence, then everyone burst out laughing, even Mr Harrison joined in. The new friends carried on eating their way through the table of food in front of them. Each of the wizards sharing stories of the old days. The wizards were happy being the centre of attention. They had a whole new audience for their stories. The king then leaned over to Ane midst one of Eric's stories.

"Young lady, do you think you could muster up some pickle? It is sweet and spicy, apparently it's a mixture of vegetables in some kind of sweet and spicy sauce tomato I think."

Ane waved her wand, and a jar of pickle appeared in front of the king. The king opened the jar and dipped in his finger. There was a smile a mile wide on his face.

"I could get used to this." The king tucked into the pickle which he knew was going to taste amazing with his pork pie

Mr Harrison had observed what had just happened. He looked at Ane with a worried look on his face. This is how it had all started in the first place; little favours for the king. This is how The Great Wars started. He didn't say anything, he just knew that he would have to keep a close eye on them all.

Ane sat back in her chair observing her friends sitting around the kings table. It had been a good day all in all.

"I could get used to this too, your majesty."

She turned to Owen who was sitting next to her.

"I can't believe we are sitting here with the king, queen, all our friends, and The Great Six. The Great Six, the most powerful wizards of all time!" Ane was smiling and, for once, so was Owen.

"Well, not the greatest, we aren't the greatest wizards of all time."

Everyone froze as Manuel spoke. He suddenly realised he had said that louder than he thought as everyone was now looking at him.

"Pardon?" Owen almost choked on his food.

Mr Harrison was now looking directly at Manuel, shaking his head from side to side. Manuel wasn't paying attention to him. He had discovered peanut butter and sausage sandwiches now, and couldn't take his eyes off them. That was far more important.

"Because, you know, the other two. There were eight and we were just... umm, this sandwich is the most amazing thing ever."

There was a loud cough from The Horrible Hipolito. Even he was trying to get Manuel's attention. There were some things that the other wizards didn't want everyone to know, things that were better left buried in the past.

"Eight wizards?" Ane wanted to know now. Her head quickly remembered the secret conversation that her grandfather was not allowed to talk about.

"Well, eight, you know, and... her! I suppose that makes nine. Ten if you count you know who. Do they crush the butter into the peanuts or the peanuts into the butter? And, the sausage melting the butter, wow, it is really amazing! How had we never thought about this before?"

"Manuel!" Mr Harrison was using his teacher's voice.

Manuel noticed that time. They all noticed that time. "Oh, but, we don't talk about it!" Manuel dropped his head and went back to his sandwich.

Ane was now looking at Mr Harrison. He was trying not to pay attention to her.

"We don't talk about it, you know, because of the *Spell*."

There was a shock across the table. Manuel had tried to mumble the last words of the sentence, well, he had tried, but like everything Manuel did, it hadn't quite turned out like he had wanted it to.

"Enough now!" Mr Harrison spoke again with his teacher's voice. This time his harsh teacher's voice. That was the end of the subject.

For a brief moment, everyone looked down, and returned to their food. Even the Horrible Hipolito wanted to get off that subject.

"Ane, you never did say how you still had magic?"

Everyone looked at Ane. Apart from Owen, they all had been wondering how one little girl had managed to keep magic when the rest of the kingdom had not.

"I think that when the spell was broken, I was just safe with my grandfather."

There were a few nods around the room, everyone seemed happy with the answer. Everyone other than The Horrible Hipolito who knew that wasn't actually an answer. Nothing or nobody should have been safe from *the Great Big Book of Everything and Cheese and Onion Sandwiches.*

"When you say safe...?"

"You know, my dear, this may be the best pickle I have ever eaten. I know it is the only pickle I have ever eaten, but it is the best. Do you think you would be able to make cold tomato soup?" The king looked so happy. He hadn't been paying attention to any of the conversations in the room, and hadn't noticed The Horrible Hipolito staring angrily at him for interrupting. He was just happy to be still eating.

"I am sure I can." Ane waved her wand, and made the king some soup.

"Ane, when you say safe?" The Horrible Hipolito insisted still wanting his answer.

"Sorry, Hipolito. Yes, safe, in my grandfather's trunk. It is magic proof."

Two of the wizards stood up suddenly, then so did three more. Eric didn't, but only because if he got off his chair and stood up, he would be lower than the table he was already sitting at.

"Grandfather's trunk?" The Horrible Hipolito had a teacher's voice now. It sounded a lot like Mr Harrison's.

Ane hadn't noticed them standing and looking at her. She was too interested in her knickerbockerglory, and the happy sounds coming from the king next to her.

"Yes, you see, he has this old trunk with some dials on it. Although I don't know why it needs dials and it has padlocks."

The wizards all looked frightened. They were sharing glances at each other; Manuel fainted.

There was a loud knock at the doors to The Great Feast Room. Everyone in turn looked at each other in wonder who it could be. Nobody was missing from the table who had been on this adventure, and the queen had left strict instructions not to let anyone else into the palace. The doors started to open, and Ane's grandfather came bursting through the doors. All the wizards, apart from Eric and Mr Harrison, grabbed their wands and pointed them out in front of them. Even Manuel, and he was unconscious. They were not going to be of any use as they didn't have any magic; it was just instinct.

"Grandfather!" Ane screamed, she was so pleased to see him. He was smiling directly at her as he walked towards the table. On purpose he was ignoring the looks from the other wizards in the room.

The big smile in Ane's face didn't last long through as everyone quickly noticed that he didn't come alone.

"Ane... Maria... Chacon!" Her mother shouted as she walked through the door.

Yes, there was no doubt about it, this was a proper three-named telling-off. At last, she now knew that running away from home and taking on the greatest wizards of all time meant she had finally reached her mother's limit, and by the look on her face it was something she would think twice about doing again...